"Years ago, I read Pen's first book and knew that she was a fine writer. She still is. The combination of impeccable research and relational and spiritual adventure is irresitible. We are in a real place wih real people. A feast of characters and ideas."

Adrian Plass, author, *The Sacred Diary* series

Other titles in the *Hawk and the Dove* series:

The Breath of Peace

PENELOPE WILCOCK

LION FICTION

Published by
Lion Hudson Limited
Wilkinson House, Jordan Hill Business Park,
Banbury Road, Oxford OX2 8DR, England
www.lionhudson.com

ISBN 978 1 78264 173 5
e-ISBN 978 1 78264 174 2

This edition 2016

Acknowledgments
Scripture quotations marked NIV taken from the Holy Bible, New
International Version Anglicised. Copyright © 1979, 1984, 2011 Biblica,
formerly International Bible Society. Used by permission of Hodder &
Stoughton Ltd, an Hachette UK company. All rights reserved. "NIV" is a
registered trademark of Biblica. UK trademark number 1448790.
Scripture quotations marked KJV taken from The Authorized (King
James) Version. Rights in the Authorized Version are vested in the
Crown. Reproduced by permission of the Crown's patentee, Cambridge
University Press.

A catalogue record for this book is available from the British Library

For my dear friend Kay Bradbury who prayed me through the writing of so many stories.

Again Jesus said, 'Peace be with you! As the Father has sent me, I am sending you.' And with that he breathed on them…
John 20:21 NIV

I am the fool whose life's been spent between what's said and what is meant.
Carrie Newcomer

If you want to create evil in the world, all you have to do is pick on a little kid.
Clay Garner

Courage does not always roar. Sometimes courage is the quiet voice at the end of the day saying, 'I will try again tomorrow.'
Mary Anne Radmacher

Today I bent the truth to be kind, and I have no regret, for I am far surer of what is kind than I am of what is true.
Robert Brault

Peace I leave with you, my peace I give unto you: not as the world giveth, give I unto you. Let not your heart be troubled, neither let it be afraid.
Jesus of Nazareth – John 14:27 KJV

Contents

The Community of
St Alcuin's Abbey

(Not all members are mentioned in *The Breath of Peace*.)

Fully professed monks

Abbot John Hazell	*once the abbey's infirmarian*
Father Chad	*prior*
Brother Ambrose	*cellarer*
Father Theodore	*novice master*
Father Gilbert	*precentor*
Father Clement	*overseer of the scriptorium*
Father Dominic	*guest master*
Brother Thomas	*abbot's esquire, also involved with the farm and building repairs*
Father Francis	*scribe*
Father Bernard	*sacristan*
Brother Martin	*porter*
Brother Thaddeus	*potter*
Brother Michael	*infirmarian*
Brother Damian	*helps in the infirmary*
Brother Cormac	*kitchener*
Brother Conradus	*assists in the kitchen*
Brother Richard	*fraterer*
Brother Stephen	*oversees the abbey farm*
Brother Peter	*ostler*
Father Gerard	*almoner*
Brother Josephus	*acted as esquire for Father Chad between abbots; now working in the abbey school*
Brother Germanus	*has worked on the farm, occupied in the wood yard and gardens*
Brother Mark	*too old for taxing occupation, but keeps the bees*

10

Brother Paulinus	*works in the kitchen garden and orchards*
Brother Prudentius	*now old, helps on the farm and in the kitchen garden and orchards*
Brother Fidelis	*now old, oversees the flower gardens*
Father James	*makes and mends robes, occasionally works in the scriptorium*
Brother Walafrid	*herbalist, oversees the brew house*
Brother Giles	*assists Brother Walafrid and works in the laundry*
Brother Basil	*old, assists the sacristan – ringing the bell for the office hours, etc.*

Fully professed monks now confined to the infirmary through frailty of old age

Father Gerald	*once sacristan*
Brother Denis	*once a scribe*
Father Paul	*once precentor*
Brother Edward	*onetime infirmarian, now living in the infirmary but active enough to help there and occasionally attend Chapter and the daytime hours of worship*

Novices

Brother Benedict	*assists in the infirmary*
Brother Boniface	*helps in the scriptorium*
Brother Cassian	*works in the school*
Brother Cedd	*helps in the scriptorium and when required in the robing room*
Brother Felix	*helps Father Gilbert*
Brother Placidus	*helps on the farm*
Brother Robert	*assists in the pottery*

Members of the community mentioned in earlier stories and now deceased

Abbot Gregory of the Resurrection

Abbot Columba du Fayel (also known as Father Peregrine)

Father Matthew	*novice master*
Brother Cyprian	*porter*
Father Aelred	*schoolmaster*
Father Lucanus	*novice master before Father Matthew*
Father Anselm	*once robe-maker*
Brother Andrew	*kitchener*

Acknowledgments

My thanks to singer-songwriter Carrie Newcomer for allowing me to use the quotation from her song at the start of this book. Musicians are notoriously sticky about allowing song quotations, and she was very gracious in permitting me to do so. Information about Carrie's work can be found at CarrieNewcomer.com.

Notes on the Text

A note from the author on fourteenth-century English...

Once or twice, in a review or a passing comment, someone has remarked that occasionally this author loses her grip on fourteenth-century English, or that a word or phrase is used that seems out of place for the fourteenth century. Because I think readers may not always immediately see what I am doing here, I thought an explanatory note might be helpful.

The Hawk and the Dove series is set in the 1300s, and if it were written in fourteenth-century English, it would read something like this:

> Fowles in the frith,
> The fisshes in the flood,
> And I mon waxe wood
> Much sorwe I walke with
> For beste of boon and blood.

Or this:

> But nathelees, whil I have tyme and space,
> Er that I ferther in this tale pace,
> Me thynketh it acordaunt to resound
> To telle yow al the condicioun
> Of ech of hem, so as it semed me,
> And whiche they weren, and of what degree,
> And eek in what array that they were inne;
> And at a knyght than wol I first bigynne.

Now, that would be fun! I would relish the challenge of employing my studies of English literature through the ages, and creating a modern novel written entirely in Middle English. The only snag would be that no one would want to read it, and even they thatte started wolde gyve up in a litel space, ywys, I wot it roghte wele.

So the challenge I took up instead of that one, was how to write novels set in the fourteenth century that allowed the modern reader to enter that world *as if it were familiar territory.*

Reading Shakespeare, and Chaucer, and the seventeenth-century poets George Herbert and John Donne, something that strikes me every time is the vivid homeliness of their language. The images are domestic and friendly, down to earth somehow, connecting the writer to readers of any era with an almost startling immediacy.

Here's Donne tackling the teasing art of seduction by writing about a flea:

Marke but this flea, and marke in this,
How little that which thou deny'st me is;
Me it suck'd first, and now sucks thee,
And in this flea our two bloods mingled bee...

And here's George Herbert, with holier matters in mind, writing in 1633, in his poem *The Elixir*, about the transformative power of undertaking lowly tasks 'for Thy sake':

A servant with this clause
Makes drudgerie divine
Who sweeps a room as for Thy laws
Makes that and th'action fine.

There is a forthrightness, an earthiness, a picturesque domesticity about the handling of language throughout the middle ages right up to the eighteenth century, at which point the age of enlightenment kicked in to make a change of emphasis.

In writing The Hawk and the Dove series, I have tried to capture not medieval *usage* of language, but medieval *flavour* – the drollery of its wit, the warmth and immediacy of its style.

In practice this means knotting and weaving modern phraseology into a net capable of catching that elusive earthy quality. So, for example, in this book (*The Breath of Peace*) there is a riff running about William's 'scary eyes'. In terms of the story, this works with the purpose of continuing the process, wrought over the course of the previous three novels, of allowing the reader to follow through deepening insight into a character whose presenting face is essentially unlikeable. Theologically, this is about redemption beginning with learning to love the unlovely – the heart of compassion and the nature of grace: 'while we were yet sinners...' (Romans 5:8). In introducing the question of the 'scary eyes', the theme of learning to see things from someone else's point of view begun in *The Hardest Thing To Do* is taken to the level of being actually behind or within the eyes of the individual whose gaze is threatening, disturbing and unsettling – and realizing that *to that person* the unnerving gaze is unintentional; and in any case he is the one person in the world who has no means of experiencing or perceiving it.

But the term 'scary' has a very modern ring to it. So the question I tossed about for a while was whether to avoid the modern idiom, or use it in this case. I decided to use it because the modern reader, familiar with it in daily speech, would grasp immediately its affectionate and less than serious application. If someone says to you, 'You have scary eyes!' they are not taking you entirely seriously – it's meant, but it's slightly teasing. The phrase originates with Madeleine in this story, and allows the reader to keep the awareness that William *has* a disquieting presence – even his wife finds him somewhat unnerving at times – while at the same time moving closer into this vulnerable and damaged person beset by the fears and shame that overrun his inner world.

'Scary' is flippant, teasing, affectionate, light, gently mocking – and, familiar with these nuances in daily speech, a reader will instantly catch these resonances. But how does this sit with a fourteenth-century context? Of course this exact use of 'scary' does not carry over from the modern day to the fourteenth century, but the flavour – the gentle mockery, the teasing – does. To use an archaic form would have the disadvantage of imparting a mannered and wooden quality to the interaction, which was precisely the thing I wanted to avoid. Madeleine speaks to William within a relationship of intimacy – an intimacy further underlined by his being a man so very hard for anyone to get close to. Use of a term stiffened by the distance of history would not do here. The idiom is modern, but used with the purpose of bringing to life for the modern reader a domestic relationship from a distant historical context.

Similarly I will use phrases like 'not the sharpest knife in the box' or 'what are you like?', 'does my head in' or 'I see where you're coming from' or 'get a grip', because there is no inherent reason why they could not have been formulated in the middle ages – they don't rely on a specific historical context in the way that 'on the level' (a phrase imported from Freemasonry) or 'all guns blazing' (obviously post-medieval) or 'nineteen to the dozen' (from the nineteenth-century Cornish tin mines) would do.

On the other hand, when one of the people working editorially on the text, for one of the earlier novels, suggested that I put in the mouth of Abbot John the words 'Are you kidding?' I rejected that instinctually, because it has the wrong flavour – it is *too* American, too modern, too specifically rooted in our contemporary world – and because there are other words – jesting, joking, etc. – that serve the exact same purpose without stepping out of the medieval world.

Modern idiom in these novels is primarily chosen where it serves the purpose of conveying nuances of relationship – because these novels are about the delicate intermingling of gritty, earthy, difficult daily relationship in community with the leavening, beautifying, fragrant threads and root-hairs of divine grace.

The great cause of writing fiction is to weave a bag to carry truth. It is a means of bringing truth home. The art of story-telling is to present a context 'long ago and far away', allowing us to examine without feeling defensive the issues that belong to our lives, our dilemmas, our day. The marriage of the far-away and the here-and-now is achieved by the use of language. The Hawk and the Dove series comes from the days of fire and stone, of ox-carts and rushlights, the days before tomatoes and potatoes were on the menu: but the stories in it are yours and mine, and what we rely on to make the bridge is the way in which language is used.

My first love as a reader and as a writer is poetry – I came only gradually to prose and have learned to love the handling of it more slowly. Thus I write first and foremost as a poet, balancing the word-music and cadences of every sentence, sitting with a thesaurus always open in search of words that convey not approximately but precisely the heart-meaning of the trail of grace I am trying to coax the reader along – until you can see it; until a man's weeping makes your belly contract with his, until his quiet joke and sly grin stays with you, and makes you smile as you remember it while you're in your kitchen chopping vegetables for your supper.

Nobody could know better than I do that I cannot always have got the balance right – that sometimes my choices of modern idiom may have been ill-advised, and my research of an immersion into the medieval and monastic world is sometimes patchy and incomplete. But it has been a study and a love affair of a lifetime, and in this series of novels I give it my best shot.

Chapter One

An owl hooted, soft and eerie, in the blackness between the dripping trees that bordered and hung menacing over the lane. She took in the sound, and then she stopped dead. That was wrong. No owl perched so low. It was a signal. It was a man. Her heart thundered, battering erratic, high in her chest. Again the low, unearthly call floated through the cold mist. Madeleine stood trembling, sick with terror, her knees shaking, unable to move. How many of them were there? Footpads? Thieves? Or worse?

She almost fainted as she saw the human clot of shadow emerge from the trees against the wall.

'Who goes there?' She tried to sound sharp and challenging, but her voice shook with undisguisable fear.

As the man came towards her, she could not run, could do nothing; blind panic stopped her throat and then in the glimmers of moonlight shining fitful through the trees she recognized a familiar outline and gait in the vague shape approaching her... 'W-W-William?' She could hardly gasp out the question.

'Oh, my sweet, did I scare you?'

And relief drained every ounce of strength from her so that she all but collapsed into his arms.

'My darling!' He was laughing at the situation, holding her close to him, laughing: 'My darling, it's only me!'

It was the laughter that did it. Incoherent rage took hold of her, and she pulled back from his arms.

'What a stupid, stupid thing to do! It isn't funny! How was I supposed to know it was you? You frightened the wits out of me! It could have been anybody standing there in the trees! Why didn't you bring a lantern anyway? What did you think you were doing, crouched in the hedgerow mooing like a cow fallen in the ditch?'

'I wasn't mooing. I was being an owl!'

'An owl? Oh, Lord! You almost scared the life out of me! All I knew, standing there in the dark, was that someone, something – some fell being, I knew not what, but no owl – was hiding in the trees! Saints alive, William de Bulmer – what kind of man are you?'

'A penitent one.' He tried to take her into his embrace again, and she would have nothing of it. He tried another tack. 'Why were you out so late, anyway? I was worried about you. That's why I came out to look for you.'

'Look, let's not stand here in the lane, shall we? It's dark, it's freezing cold, it's wet, and I'll bet you've let the fire go out!'

'Madeleine…' His hand found hers. 'Don't be cross with me. I didn't mean to scare you. I didn't think.'

She allowed him to hold her hand, but he felt no returning pressure of affection. The silence that emanated from her as they splashed through the mud and puddles of the rutted lane felt icier than the raw February night.

William cursed himself. To come upon an unidentified man waiting for her on the lonely road home would have been terrifying. Madeleine never spoke about the night the villagers had come for her and her mother, burned their cottage to the ground, killed or stole their livestock and left her mother dead and Madeleine stunned and bleeding. But she never mentioned it because she wanted to keep the horror sealed away, not because she'd forgotten. And he should have realized. Should have been more thoughtful. As they trudged without speaking the last few yards to their gate, he tried desperately to remember if he had in fact thought to build up the fire before he set out. It was difficult to think. More anxiously pressing was the increasing certainty that he had forgotten to shut the hens in. This he dared not admit.

They walked in silence until they came to the stone walls that encircled their homestead, Caldbeck Cottage. He opened the gate and stood aside for her to enter, latching it securely behind them.

He had a bad feeling that she was probably right about the fire. He had taken scraps of left-over bread and vegetables to their sow, Lily, mixed in with her oat mash along with the buttermilk from the morning, and a few apples from the store. He had milked Marigold, Madeleine's much-loved goat brought with her from St Alcuin's. He spread fresh straw in her stall, in the pig sty, and in the palfrey's stable, when he fastened them in for the night. The animals had no need of mucking out. At the beginning and end of the short months of summer – in May and in September – they cleaned out the animal housing, but through the long cold months of the northern winter the build-up of litter on the floor offered a valuable source of warmth, and made the food go further – a cold animal is a hungry one. The goat's housing and the stable smelt sweet; the odour of their dung was not offensive. William felt less sure about the fragrance of a pig.

The trips across from the hay barn and the straw barn made extra work. Madeleine had wanted to store some bales in the goat shed and above the stable, but William had adamantly refused. There had been an argument about that as well, he recalled.

'No,' he had said: 'absolutely not. The hay cannot be stored in the same building with the straw, and neither one in the same building with the beasts. And the hay store cannot even be near the straw, or the beasts, or the house. It only takes one bale, just one damp bale, to combust, and we lose the hay, the straw, the beasts and the house if they are all cheek by jowl. It must be separate. No, Madeleine! It *must* be.'

'William, you're being too particular. It's not a great farm! And anyway, we won't be buying damp hay, we'll be choosy, we'll check. It's just so much work traipsing back and forth all weathers to lug it in.'

'I am *not* being too particular. If we inadvertently roast that goat something tells me you, for one, won't be able to face eating her for supper. And we rely on the milk. Yes, we have enough money on deposit if we live frugally. We can hope to build up and increase what we have here, and we shall prosper. It would take only one fire to dash our hopes and dreams, and set back by several years everything we've planned. I've known barn fires, and seen the wind take them across the thatches of one building after another, wreaking devastation. We can't make ourselves safe against everything, but not doing what we can is just madness.'

'I still think you're making a mountain out of a molehill. I've husbanded animals all my life and always kept a few bales in with the beasts. It helps keep them warm, for one thing. I've never had a fire, not once.'

He looked at her. 'What are you talking about? Your house burnt down.'

Irritation twitched her face. This thrust annoyed her intensely. 'Aye, and yours did too, wherever you kept your dratted hay! That's not the point.'

And so it had continued, back and forth, for the best part of an afternoon: but he would not budge. When they moved in, he had not the skills to build and thatch a hovel for storing hay, so a precious portion of their money had been spent on hiring a handy neighbour to do that for them. The incident had made William feel suddenly defenceless and lonely. The shared skills of a monastic community of men had made for great strength and security. Leaving that behind at the age of fifty with very little experience of mending and building made him very vulnerable by comparison with everything he had known so far, even if they had inherited an income as well as a house. This was what made him so adamant about the hay store. This house and money that had been left them represented the chance of a lifetime. It would not come again. He knew he would never be able to live with himself if he stood watching impotently as flames reached the thatch of his home, and he with no means of fighting it but himself, his wife, a well and a small stack of leather buckets. He refused to take the risk.

'Nobody ever thinks they're buying damp hay,' he insisted. 'Nobody goes to the farm and says, "Ooh, that's cheap, must be damp, I'll have it all." It takes you by surprise. That's why it pays to be cautious. It's not the things you know are going to happen that ruin a man, it's the things that catch him out.'

'What?' she snapped. 'You mean, like spending the entire fortune of an abbey on a ship not safe in harbour and watching it go to the bottom of the sea?' It was an unkind dig, raking up his past mistakes, and she felt a pang of guilt even as she said it and watched him turn his face away, stung by the taunt.

'Aye,' he replied quietly, after a moment's silence: 'exactly like that. Well, let's not do it again. I haven't been lucky with risks.'

Not even the risk of leaving a lifetime spent in monastic life to get married, he thought bitterly as he followed his wife into the house on this February night. Oh, the love between them was sweet at times, and no amount of spats between them came anywhere near denting the basic reality that he adored her: but it had been a very long time since his everyday life had brought him so many scoldings, and led him so inexorably into one kind of trouble after another.

He thought if he let her go first up to bed, he could slip out quietly to the henhouse and close it for the night. Even if (as was most likely) the fox had been at dusk and taken a bird, that would not become apparent until morning, and he could pretend he just hadn't noticed the evening before. 'They were already roosting,' he could say. 'I couldn't tell how many were in.'

That would bring wrath on his head too, because her immediate rejoinder would be: 'If you couldn't tell how many were in, you might have left some shut out. You must count them! You must count them in every time!'

He slipped past her at the door as she bent to unfasten her pattens (the wooden clogs that kept the all-pervasive winter wet out of her boots) and went in ahead of her to attend to the fire. He found it almost dead. He had been longer out looking for her in the lane than he expected. Only a few tiny embers remained. He tore a fragment of lint from the small supply of it they had close by the hearth, drew the embers together, laid the scrap of charred linen over them and built above that a careful pyramid of dry sticks, balancing on top of everything a stiff dribble of candle wax they had saved. He bent low and blew patiently on the embers until the smoking scrap of fabric caught light. And then he prayed. He stayed on his knees, apparently watching the beginnings of the fire, but in reality he prayed. 'Please,' his heart whispered: 'Just this once. Please let the wretched thing take.' And it did. The sticks were dry enough, the lint scrap large enough, the embers just hot enough, and the remnant of wax proved adequate as it melted to give the necessary extra boost. As the kindling wood took light he added the next size up of split wood, carefully positioning the pieces. He had his fire. 'Thank you,' he said in the silence of his soul, 'for sparing me that.'

He got up from his knees to fetch the pot still half-full of stew from last night's supper, and set it low on the hook to warm through. His wife had hung her cloak on the nail and taken through to the pantry the bag of provisions she had walked into the town to buy, this having been market day.

'Well, at least I see you cleaned the hens' feeding bucket out this time when you shut them in,' she said as she came to the fireside. The adrenalin rush of the fear she had felt in the lane, and its following sea of anger, had ebbed away now. Madeleine, left feeling flat and slightly guilty in its wake, thought she'd better look for something positive to say. She glanced at her husband, but he did not reply. He stirred the stew with more attention than it deserved and kept his eyes on the pot.

'William? You – you did feed the hens, didn't you? You did shut them in?'

He made no reply. She thought at first he was angry with her, and felt irritated with him for being so petty – after all, it was his fault she'd had such a scare, he shouldn't have been hanging about in the hedge playing the fool. Madeleine glared at him in frustration. And then some instinct took her past her first assumptions through to the reality. Her eyes widened.

'You haven't fed them at all, have you? You forgot all about them. You haven't shut them in!'

Still he did not look at her, but he felt the force of her gaze on him like wind and fire, just as clear and honest and direct as her brother's eyes, and just as capable of the most fiery indignation. William recognized a moment of truth when it came towards him. He abandoned the self-protective lie half formed in his mind. But his mouth went dry.

'I was scared to tell you,' he admitted, his voice so low she could hardly make out the words. She stared at him in disbelief, then whirled about, snatched up the half loaf from the table, struggled her pattens back onto her feet; then the door slammed behind her as she disappeared out into the night once more.

William fetched the bowls and spoons for their supper, wondered whether to follow her but thought better of it, and sat down by the fire he had made, to wait miserably for her return. She was gone longer than throwing bread into the henhouse and bolting its door could have taken. It came as no surprise when she flung open the door and stood there leaning on one hand against the frame as she pulled off her clogs, the corpses of two hens dangling reproachfully by their feet from her other hand. She spared her husband no glance, but stalked through into the scullery and hung the birds on a rafter nail to be dealt with in the morning.

She came back in silence then to the fireside, stopping at the table to pick up their bowls. She set one down on the hearth, stirring the pot, then ladling barely warm stew into first one bowl, which she thrust in her husband's direction with neither a word nor a look, then the other, with which she retreated to the far side of their table.

William received his bowl from her humbly. Never had he felt less like eating, though he'd been hungry enough an hour before. He dared not refuse the food, dared not even raise his eyes to her or thank her when she gave him the dish. He took it, and in silence they ate the tepid stew with the little white discs of congealed fat barely melted. William felt sick at the sight of it, but he ate it. When they were finished, he took her bowl along with his through to the room on the back of the house that did for storage and scullery and preparation space, scooped some water out of the tubful that stood near the door, swilled one bowl into the other, swilled the second bowl round, then opened the window and flung the swill-water into the night. That would have to do until morning. Some grease left on the bowls and spoons wouldn't hurt; they could be scoured along with the pot the next day.

He left them on the table there and returned with slow reluctance into their living room. He had a strip of hide cut for a belt, and wanted to make holes in it for the buckle. He took it, along with the spike to make the holes and a stool from the table, to the fireside where his wife sat in angry silence thinking about hens. The spike was too blunt. One end hurt his hand as he tried to push it through, the other end slipped and punctured the palm of his other hand, though it had completely failed to make more than a mark on the leather. He swore and sucked the bruised and bleeding place, while Madeleine watched him moodily, too cross with him even to point out he'd do better with the bradawl than a simple spike. She thought he ought to know that anyway.

Some evenings, as they sat by their fire through the winter darkness, Madeleine, her carding or spinning done for the day, would lift down her vielle from where it hung on the wall to play the folk songs and ballads of childhood remembrance, and William loved that. It was evidently not going to be one of those evenings. Even the fire was sulking. The wind was wrong.

Eventually they gave up on the day, and Madeleine stood holding the candle while William tidied the fire together, and then followed her up to bed.

They undressed in silence. It was too cold to sleep naked. William kept his undershirt on, and his socks. The sheepskins spread on their mattress under the linen sheet made their bed warmer as well as softer, and the fire in the room below kept the winter damp from their chamber. Even so he shivered as he slipped between the sheets. Their bed felt distinctly inhospitable. Madeleine said nothing, and did not turn toward him for their usual goodnight kiss.

William lay rigid in the cold bed at her side, longing for her to hold him, longing for this to be over now and forgiven, for mistakes to be allowable, for things to be simple and just all right. His hand throbbed where the spike had pierced it. He felt cold and wretched and completely forlorn.

'*What?*' said Madeleine, sudden and fierce into the darkness, acutely aware of William's frozen silence, angry with him for having the temerity to exude this chill on top of everything else. '*What's the matter?*'

Bewildered, William wondered what he could possibly reply to this. She knew what was wrong. He had frightened her without meaning to in the lane. He had let the fire go too low to heat their supper. He had forgotten the hens and let the fox take two more precious birds. He was in total disgrace. He tried to frame some kind of understanding that would allow him to see why she was asking him what was the matter.

'Just grow up!' Her voice shook with passion, and she kept it low with an effort. 'I know why *I'm* angry, but I can't see that you have anything to be so resentful about! What's wrong with you?'

Grow up... The words fastened on to William. Hearing this he recognized what was happening. It had been an occurrence of almost monotonous regularity in his childhood and his early years in monastic life as a novice. Others being angry about the original misdemeanour was never enough for them. There followed the complicated matter of his own response. If he kept his body still and his face without expression, he was mulish, insolent, insubordinate. If he attempted any kind of remonstration, he provoked indignation and outrage. If he lowered his eyes or turned his head away, he was sulking. If he tried to behave normally, he was indifferent and insensitive or unrepentant. If he kept his expression and tone carefully neutral, he was rebellious or cold or rude. And if in the end he was reduced to tears, he was snivelling... self-piteous... complaining... attention-seeking. He wondered how often in the first decade of his life the threat of 'If you don't stop that grizzling, I'll give you something to cry about!' had screamed and raged around his head. It was happening again now. Someone was angry with him for perpetuating his crimes by continuing to exist. Nothing he said would be right. Even here in bed at night he was in the wrong because his wakefulness had been detected. And he had no doubt that if he'd fallen asleep his callousness would have been unforgiveable. He had no alternative but to ride this out as best he could.

Madeleine heard his breathing change from his nose to his mouth. She felt his cautious movement, and saw in the moonlight, as she turned her head to glare at him, the surreptitious wiping of his eyes with the heel of his hand. Impatient with this, she turned her face away again. He deserved to be in trouble. How could he be so thoughtless and so careless – *all the time?*

Careful to minimize any disturbance he might make, William turned over on his side, with his back to her. Madeleine lay in the frigid darkness, furious about the hens, and doubly furious because she could feel the tremor of his misery. She didn't want to have to deal with that, or pretend his incompetence didn't matter after all. A long time passed. The night was very cold.

Eventually, exasperated, all hope of sleep exiled completely, Madeleine rolled over to him. She felt his body tense as she laid her hand on his arm.

'William…'

He did not move, but she knew without doubt that he lay painfully awake.

'William, come back to me.'

There was nothing wheedling, nothing coaxing in her voice. Not one corner of Madeleine's spirit lent itself to accommodating other people's petulance or moods.

'William.'

He turned over again to face her. She took him in her arms.

'I'm sorry I spoke so sharp,' she said simply. He shook his head, past speaking, and she held him close to her. The hopelessness and despair in him had its talons into his gut, and he clung to her desperately. She realized then that he had not been angry with her at all, only terribly ashamed and needing to be forgiven. Her body relaxed and softened, and she lifted her hand to stroke his head as she cradled him. 'It's all right,' she whispered, soothing him. 'It's all right…'

'I know it's not the same, but I'll get you some more hens,' he eventually managed to say.

She kissed the end of his nose, as light as a butterfly. 'Moorhens' eggs taste of mud,' she teased him gently: 'let's stick to chickens.'

With peace restored between them, Madeleine resigned herself to accept the depredations of the fox, and held her husband in her arms until she gradually dozed off and her embrace slackened and released as she drifted into sleep.

William lay awake, his mind still battered by the tumult of emotion.

Barely more than a year ago, his body lapped in peace, lying entwined in afterglow of love, when they were first married, he had felt all fear, all shame, slip out of his soul. Everything had just been all right. That was then. In the intervening time, the householder's round had taken its toll. William was well used to people holding him in contempt and being angry with him, finding him a source of outrage and indignation; but never since his childhood had his intelligence been found wanting. Domestic life had made him into a dunce; and he hated that.

He lay without moving, aware of the sound of the wind blustering about the roof, of the smell of herbs and stew and woodsmoke and cured hams that pervaded their house, of the warm presence of his wife beside him in the bed, her breath whistling slightly. He was glad she didn't snore – or not very often. He lay still, his mind seething with memories, his heart in turmoil. He felt relieved they had ended the day on speaking terms at least, but it had left him with a confusion of shame and self-loathing and hurt that he couldn't begin to sort out. He remained alert in every sense the whole night through, and by the time the sun rose he felt weary beyond description. Desiring no interaction of any kind at all, he slipped out of bed quietly, leaving Madeleine to sleep on as he crept downstairs. If he walked on the edges of the treads, they barely creaked at all.

He raked the ashes and found enough life left to revive a fire. Their money had stretched far enough to buy a second good-sized iron pot. He unhooked last night's stew and sniffed it. The smell of it this morning had become less than inviting.

He carried it through to their scullery to take out to the sow. The pitiful sight of their dead hens hung by their feet from the rafters sent a fresh shaft of guilt, like an icicle used as a weapon, stabbing through his belly. He averted his eyes from them, measuring out a cup of oatmeal, a cup of milk and two cups of well-water into the other pot to begin breakfast. He added a generous pinch of salt, took the pot through to the fire, and hooked it up onto the chains. He fetched one of several long-handled wooden spoons to give the porridge a stir as it began to seethe over the fire. This spoon was of his own making, his first foray into shaping wood. Madeleine said he had made the bowl of it too shallow to be very useful, but he had felt proud to have made it nonetheless – at the time. It seemed a clumsy, graceless piece of workmanship when he looked at it again this morning.

The porridge would take a while. He scraped the remnants of yesterday's pottage into an earthenware dish, and took it out to the pigsty. Later, one of them would drive Lily out into the forest, where she could scavenge what little remained of beechmast and acorns, beetles, slugs and fungi and anything else that would take her fancy under the rattling canopy of bare winter twigs below the steel-grey sky. For now, Lily immersed her snout happily in their left-overs, devouring them greedily.

The sun had scarcely cleared the rim of the hills, and the light of its rising still reflected crimson on the underbelly of heavy clouds. The ground was muddy where it had thawed here and there, but the days still continued cold enough to hold the land as if it had been banded by a wheelwright. It had not got so soft as to make it slippery or slow to walk over. Ice still fringed the puddles.

Back in the cottage, William stirred the porridge again to prevent it sticking, fetched the tub of honey and two bowls and spoons to the table, and took a bucket of water and the milk pail across to Marigold's stable, where she waited impatiently, reared up with her front hooves on the rim of her stall. The hay in her net had all gone. He led her out to the milking block, and she jumped up willingly, knowing her routine. Even so he chained her. Nothing in him trusted a goat to co-operate reliably.

He had flung a generous handful of barley and another of oatmeal into a crock, and this he tipped into her bowl, washing down her udder without delay, before she got bored. He took no more than half a can of milk from her this morning. She would be kiddling late, her milk would just take them through the worst of the winter, but until someone's milk-cows calved in March he could see they would have a few lean weeks to go through with no milk at all. They would be pulling in their belts for a while. Especially now they had lost two more hens – if indeed it proved on inspection to be no more than two.

This year, he thought, they should try to afford a second milch goat. Even if the kid Marigold carried in her belly turned out to be female, nothing would come of that this coming year. With a second fully grown animal they could alternate breeding and milking through.

The browsing was almost non-existent now, and most of the evergreens did even goats no good. William tethered Marigold with care where he judged her busy teeth could do no lasting damage in stripping bark from the trees, promising to come back with some kale stalks from the leavings later on. He took a minute to scratch her bony head, and Marigold butted him in return; affectionately, but painfully.

William paused to pluck a sprig of rosemary as he hastened back to the house. He left the precious yield of milk in the scullery to deal with later, while he stirred the porridge, now thick enough to eat. He decided to leave the palfrey and the hens until he had called Madeleine to eat. They needed attention, but he thought burnt porridge would not bless the morning.

He ran light up the stairs to their bedroom, where he found the bedclothes folded back neatly that the mattress might air, and his wife already almost dressed although only half awake.

'Breakfast,' he said, and she nodded still sleepily, saying nothing, absorbed in lacing her kirtle. She couldn't understand it. The strings seemed shorter than they used to be.

William retreated down the stairs and ladled out their porridge, as it had now reached a critical stage and he could smell it just starting to burn. He lifted the pot off the fire and set it down on the hearth. Just before he sat down to eat, he found the thick, squat earthenware jug for making hot drinks, dipped it full of well-water from the pail in the scullery, and left it at the fireside to heat. He dropped in it the sprig of rosemary and a hot stone, which he lifted with tongs from the heart of the fire and blew free of ashes before he set it into the jug.

Madeleine joined him as he sat down at the table.

She sniffed the steam that rose from the porridge appraisingly. 'A bit burnt,' she commented. She opened the tub of honey and dug some out with her spoon. 'Well? How many hens have we left?'

'I haven't been to the hens yet,' her husband replied, trying a spoonful of the porridge. He agreed with her. He had been too late to stop it catching, and now it tasted burnt.

'Haven't – William, are you serious? You haven't been to see how many hens are left?'

William took another spoonful of porridge. 'I've been doing other things.'

'Other things? What could be more important than checking the hens, after you knew the fox had been in there last night? And you ought to take honey with your porridge, it's good for you.'

'I don't like porridge with honey on it. I don't like honey at all. I know it's important to check the hens, but it's important to get the fire going and make breakfast and milk the goat and tether

her out to get what little there is to eat while it's not dark. And feed the pig.'

'It doesn't matter if you don't like honey, you should still eat it; it keeps colds away. And the goat isn't so important now she's drying off. I would have gone to the hens first.'

Her husband put down his spoon. 'Checking the hens,' he said quietly, 'was not your priority. Staying in bed was.'

'Oh, William, for goodness' sake! Don't be so petty! What's the matter, are you all full of churning resentment just because I slept in and you had to make the breakfast for a change? Well, I should have got up, shouldn't I, because you burnt it anyway. Where are you going now?'

William had got up from the table, taking his bowl of porridge with him. In the pantry he took the wooden lid from the crock of barley grain and scooped a handful, which he dropped into his porridge, replacing the lid of the jar with quiet precision.

'To feed the hens,' he replied, as he came back through the room where Madeleine sat staring at him in astonishment as he passed. 'There's tea in the pot if you want it.'

'Oh, don't be ridiculous, William! Honestly, you're always so touchy about everything! And for mercy's sake put your pattens over your boots – you'll ruin them if you go out in this weather like –'

He latched the door behind him with the same quiet precision he had used to put back the lid on the crock of barley.

'– that.' Shaking her head in disbelief, Madeleine turned her attention to her breakfast again. It was, she acknowledged, not badly burned. It still tasted good, especially with honey on it from bees that gathered nectar from the herbs and blossoms in the garden. It tasted different from the abbey's honey; their bees concentrated on the moorland heather.

She finished her porridge and went to the fireside to pour herself a mug of fragrant rosemary tea. While she was there, she added a couple of small logs to the fire. She wondered whether to pour a cup for William too, but thought it better to leave it where it would keep hot.

By the hearth, Madeleine had a low chair with a sheepskin on it, where she sat in the evenings, and there she took her cup of tea now, to drink peacefully by the fire. Despite the loss of her hens and her husband's incomprehensible moods, life felt good. She considered the tasks of the day waiting to be done. Just as soon as she'd finished her tea she would put some dried peas to soak, and some barley. It was hard to tell from indoors exactly how the weather might be, but rays of sunlight shone in through their small windows. William had taken down the shutters. He knew she liked the sun. Some people didn't bother, and left them shut all winter – old habits died hard, and everyone had done that before they had glass. But William would put them up in the evening and take them down in the morning every day. And they hardly ever closed the shutters to their bedroom, only in a gale: they both loved the light of the moon.

She sipped her tea. Rosemary… for strengthening joy and love in the soul, for the heart and the flow of blood in the veins… for cheerfulness, vitality and peace… William loved the scent of it; he said it smelled clean and healthy. Madeleine closed her eyes, her hands warm around the heat of the cup of tea in her lap. So peaceful.

Outside the house, William had taken his bowl of porridge and the barley grain to their henhouse. Made of clapboard and raised off the ground to discourage the inevitable attention of rats, it had been built big enough for ten birds, a dozen at a squeeze. Three weeks ago their flock had been eight in number, enough to keep them in eggs and sell a few as well. A visit in broad daylight from a hungry fox had taken the number down to six. He hoped he would still find four this morning, and the two corpses Madeleine had retrieved last night would be their only losses. He could hear the sound of them crooning and muttering inside.

He set his bowl on the ground and slid back the hatch. Two birds emerged, lurching eagerly across the trodden earth around their hut to peck at the warm porridge and grain.

Despondently, William unlatched the bigger door located at the rear of the henhouse for cleaning it out. He lifted the hinged lid of the nest boxes. The other two birds were missing. He considered going back to the house to add the protection of pattens to his boots, and rejected the idea. Aware that his patience had been frayed to the point of giving way, he thought it might be preferable if he and Madeleine went their separate ways for the morning.

He picked up the board by the pigsty and opened the stout, well-fitted gate to let Lily out. Deft now at managing the tricky business of driving a pig, he guided her across their land to the woodland at its borders, where she would forage all day until the inviting rattle of the pail called her home as the light went off the afternoon when the sun began to sink in the west. William didn't really like his sow foraging on common land. She was too valuable an animal. But Madeleine had views on this. Every other homesteader kept her sow in the sty after she had bred and until she had farrowed, once the best of the autumn fodder had been taken from the forest floor. But Madeleine said the lack of exercise was bad for a sow, making farrowing harder. The winter days were short; Lily went out late and came in early – but out she did go; Madeleine insisted upon it.

As he walked across to the edge of the woods, William's eyes roved here and there for any sign of their missing hens. Just on the fringe of the woodland he spotted one forlorn corpse. Evidently the fox had left it there for later. He bent and picked it up by its cold yellow feet curled in death and turned to go home, leaving Lily rooting contentedly under the trees.

Aware of his mood darkening to something like entrenched bitterness, and unable to lift it despite determined effort and the clear brightness of the morning with its blackbird song and catkins coming on the trees, William trudged back to the house. The soft, heavy weight of the dead bird hung from his hand, the wind-ruffled feathers kissing his skin, the loose hanging head at the end of the broken neck dangling and bobbling and nagging at his knees with every step. He laid the corpse he carried on the roof of the henhouse, temporarily, while he went for an armful of hay to set down within Marigold's reach, and another for his palfrey. He filled her hayrack, but by this time the winter wet had seeped through the layers of leather that soled his boots, and his feet were freezing. He retrieved the dead hen, and carried it indoors, hoping Madeleine would have found something else to occupy her by now.

She stood at the table kneading dough as he came through the door. The sight of her there went through him like a blade. This was a scene he had imagined as he hungered and longed for her, suffered and yearned to make her his own when, as a monk at St Alcuin's Abbey, that dream seemed impossible. That they might have a cottage somewhere, a place to call home, and he could come in through his own front door and find her kneading dough for their daily bread. What had not been part of his imaginings was a dead hen in one hand and an intractable pattern of domestic bickering.

'Oh, no! Another one! We have only three left, then?'

'Two,' he said, miserably. 'I haven't been able to find the other one. I guess the fox took her. This one was all the way across to the wood. Whether he killed it there or dragged it to have by for a larder I couldn't say. I'm sorry, Madeleine. I'm really sorry.'

He sounded sombre, his face morose as he went through to hook the dead bird up from the rafters with her sisters.

'Is there any tea left?' He came through to the fireside, sat in the low chair Madeleine had vacated and picked up the empty mug from the hearth. He wanted to be by himself, but his feet were so cold they hurt badly and his boots were wet through. The fireside offered a solution to both problems. He poured himself a cup of the tepid tea, and replenished the fire with the last of the wood in the basket.

'We're low on kindling, too,' he commented. 'I'll split some more in a minute. I'll just have this.'

His wife watched the steam rising from his boots as he sat in the chair and stretched his feet towards the fire-glow.

She couldn't help making the observation: 'I did say you should've worn the pattens.'

'You did, and I heard you, and I was an idiot, and will you kindly shut up about it now?'

She continued her kneading. The silence between them did not feel friendly.

Eventually she felt the dough turn pliable and then silky under her hands. She gave it a little more time, and then returned it to the huge, beautiful terracotta bowl with the creamy glaze, that Brother Thaddeus had made, and John to their astonishment and delight had given them for a wedding present. They had not expected a wedding gift. As abbot of the community, her brother had flagrantly transgressed in offering to consecrate the marriage of a renegade monk from his own flock. The kindness of a wedding gift went beyond anything they might have expected, and they cherished it all the more because of that. Madeleine covered the dough with a wet cloth, taking the bowl and setting it on the hearthstone for the bread to rise.

'What's still to do outdoors?' she asked.

William shrugged. 'I want to brush down the horse, and they all need fresh water. Not much else. There's always something needs doing, isn't there, but nothing for you to bother with unless you want to. I should think you've enough to be getting on with in here. And it's still cold out. Wind's sharp.'

She stood looking down at him and, despite the dour set to his face this morning, thought it safe to risk an affectionate ruffling of his hair.

'Well, take those boots off before you go out again,' she chided kindly. 'It'll take those hours to dry, not to mention you'll get chilblains going out in wet boots in this cold and sticking your feet right close to the blaze like that – yes, you *will*. You can take that look off your face! Set your boots in yon chimney corner there; I'll stuff a cloth in them so they dry in shape. Give your feet a good rub down and put two pairs of thick stockings on; wear your clogs.'

William hated wooden clogs with a passion, but not as much as he hated being told what to do. And he had very little appetite for feeling foolish while somebody else lectured him with what was perfectly obvious, that he should have had the sense to do for himself.

'Madeleine, leave me alone,' he answered quietly.

She frowned, baffled. There seemed to be no shifting of the black mood that had settled on him. 'Well, I will,' she said, 'but don't you be such a numskull then. Take care of your boots and take care of your feet. We've no money for more of one and God's broken the mould for the other. Think!'

William clenched his jaw hard shut to prevent himself replying. He set down the mug of tea half-finished and bent forward to untie his boots, which he removed and set exactly where Madeleine had said, to forestall further comment. He undid the strips of cloth that fastened his stockings in place, for they were wet too, and peeled them off, laying them on the hearthstone to dry. His feet still felt cold, and he wanted to toast them by the fire for a few minutes, but his wife was still watching and he knew she was perfectly right about the chilblains. So he contented himself with briefly rubbing his toes in his hands, and then picked up the sock ties and reluctantly left the hearth to climb the stairs in search of dry stockings to put on. It was a mercy they would indeed be dry too, he reflected. At St Alcuin's monastery in this weather, the only dry clothes would be what men were wearing.

There, damp seeped right into the stones, and the cold was bone-freezing. Here in the cottage the fire warmed everything through. The chimney rose up through the middle of the house, and the other two rooms downstairs had the edge taken off the chill even with the doors shut. But they lived almost entirely in this main room through the winter, and the rising warmth also reached their bedroom, linked by the open staircase, as well as the warmth of the chimney by the head of their bed.

Obediently he further chafed his cold feet with the edge of the blanket, to restore circulation, and found two pairs of thick woollen socks to put on one over the other. He tied them in place, and rummaged in the chest for his hood to keep the cold out of his ears. 'You're not fat enough,' Madeleine commented sometimes. 'It's your own fault you're always so cold. You don't eat enough. You're forever wandering off and not finishing your food.'

It had been William's habit through three decades of monastic life to find refuge in order and control. He had wrapped the predictable, unvarying routine of liturgy and work and silence around him like a blanket. To say it had brought him peace would be inaccurate, but it had offered respite and a means of stemming chaos. When, on an unexpected impulse of yearning that had grown out of watching Abbot John's face and observing the life at St Alcuin's, he had been moved to un-shutter his heart and invite in the living Christ, everything had changed. He had imagined improvement. He had imagined at last a capacity to love, gentleness in him strengthened, and the streak of ruthless cruelty that ran through him, like a glittering black seam in a rock, chiselled out. He had been unprepared for a return to vulnerability, bringing emotions that connected in turn to memories he would prefer to forget forever. Certainly he, who had regarded women as creatures of no use to him, and therefore of less interest than the cattle on the priory grange, had never expected to fall in love.

They say love is an affair of the heart. William felt, in letting its longings lead him forth from the safe cleft in the rock where he had sheltered to the uncertain ground of domestic life, that it had opened up his heart and his gut and probably his liver and kidneys for good measure. The turbulence and difficulty of the everyday, in its present form, hooked onto the memories of household norms in the period of his life before he had entered religion, and brought to the surface memory after buried memory to torment his waking mind and harass his dreams. Incidents he had locked down in irons and refused the light of day had come straggling into conscious recollection and muddled together with his interactions with Madeleine, opening him up painfully and pitilessly to despair and self-loathing he had thought was settled and done with. As he sat pulling on his stockings, one pair over another, and folding them and lacing them carefully round his feet and legs, his soul seemed to be in danger of disembowelment. Something savage and desperate battened down in him in self-defence.

He padded soft-foot down the stairs in his socks. His wife, seated on a stool close by the window mending a difficult tear in his loose-woven russet hemp smock that he loved, lifted her head from her task to watch him push his feet into the wooden overshoes. Whether socks and pattens would suffice against the mud and wet grass she felt unsure. She thought of his best boots upstairs, but decided he had better save those for going to Mass and for when they had any kind of business abroad that required respectable appearance – which happened not often, it was true, but occasionally. So she said nothing, just observed the grim, dogged set to his face, and realized that he neither spoke to her nor looked at her – not because other things were on his mind but because right now he could bear no more of her company: which felt unjust.

William latched the door quietly and carefully behind him. Hating the inflexibility of clogs, and their tendency to turn the ankle so that walking in them was an occupation of itself requiring vigilance, he longed for the barefoot days of summer. He trudged along the path round the house to the woodshed, then stopped and swore under his breath. He'd forgotten the basket. Retracing his steps, he found it set out on the doorstep. Evidently Madeleine had noticed he'd forgotten it as well.

The woodshed, with its dusty quiet fragrance, offering shelter from the wind, was a sanctuary William appreciated. He took off the loathed pattens, and fetched the whet-stone and the hand-axe. Patiently he ground the blade until it was sharp enough to satisfy him, then he took three logs from the pile and sat on the ground with a log held in his hand in the space between his knees, and began steadily to reduce it to fine kindling sticks.

The rhythmic, methodical work felt soothing, but there was not enough in it to keep his mind busy, and before long the old memories that had all somehow got out of their dungeon began to creep up into consciousness with their sour reek of humiliation and soul-destroying shame. One by one he pushed them away, persisting with the rhythmic, gentle chop and split as the sharpened axe bit through the unresisting wood.

A boyhood memory surfaced of one day among many leaving him knocked to the floor while the blurred drunken voice of his father roared in rage for him to get to his feet and take it like a man, and he had been lost between fear of the consequences of obeying or of disobeying. That particular day he had tried to get up and been kicked off balance before he was properly on his feet, falling against the corner of the table. Even the furniture of the house had something against him, and the spiteful point of the corner hurt the soft part of his body agonizingly. Collapsing again in a sea of pain, the immoderate cackle of mocking laughter had cascaded round his senses like bright leaves of molten hate, as he tried and failed to find some vestige of self-respect and dignity to hold on to.

William did not pause in his present task. He placed each stick freed from the old log on the pile of wood dealt with, and went on to the next. Something in his belly squirmed and bucked in protest against the unbearable memories, but he held himself calm by sheer determined self-discipline, persevering doggedly with the job in hand.

He had almost finished the last of the three logs when Madeleine appeared in the doorway. He looked up at her, in time to catch the mystified expression on her face dissolve into laughter. 'What on earth are you doing it like that for?'

'Doing what like what?' He sounded none too pleased to see her.

'Sitting on the floor to split wood.'

'I'm comfortable like this. I've got the job done – what more do you want, and what business is it of yours anyway?'

'Oh! I beg your pardon! None at all! You can split wood standing on your head for all I care. Only most people would want to be bending over the task to let the force of their weight help with the chopping.'

'Fine. But not me. Is that what you came out to tell me – that I'm splitting the wood wrong as well as everything else – or did you have something further that you wanted of me?'

William did not raise his voice when he was angry. He spoke softly always, but when she annoyed him his tone assumed a dangerous quality that sounded menacing and implacably hostile. It disturbed her, and put her on the defensive.

'Have it your own way. What do I know? And I came out to see if you'd got the kindling ready because I want to heat up the bread oven and I need small sticks for that – and we have none left indoors.'

Without replying, he gathered up the stack of split wood and dropped it into the basket, then stood up and handed it to her.

'Thank you,' she said, and her tone had become distinctly

chilly. He had irritated her now. 'Can you do some more, then, so we have enough for later? This will all get used up firing the oven.'

'Yes,' he said curtly, with a small nod. She sighed. This wasn't necessary. It shouldn't be like this. Why was he so impossible?

'William –'

'Just leave me alone!' he snapped. 'For mercy's sake, leave me in peace!'

She stood a moment longer with the basket, then wheeled about and marched back down the path, offended and hurt.

Left alone in the woodshed, William took three more logs from the pile. He thought Madeleine would probably be right about bending over the wood to chop it, which made him the more determined to do it his own way. He resumed the rhythm of cutting and splitting, but it no longer felt soothing. Like guts spilling out of an animal taken down by predators, memories tumbled unchecked out of their storehouse, merciless, maddening. He concentrated on cutting the sticks fine, as narrow and slender as he could. It made a focus. But the last log had a knot in it and wouldn't split at all. He got into an absurd and mindless battle with it, determined to get the better of it and reduce it to sticks as small as splinters. With an almighty whack he drove the axe a little way into it, and there it stuck. Getting up onto his knees, he picked up the axe with the log fixed tight on the end of it, and smacked the whole thing twice without result on the ground. The third time the axe handle broke. Almost out of his mind with rage and misery, William gathered up the pile of sticks he had completed and, without stopping to put his clogs back on his feet, walked back to the house in his socks. Struggling with the door latch, he dropped the sticks in the puddle of water on the worn stone step. As he bent with iron patience to gather them again, Madeleine, having heard the latch rattle, opened the door from inside.

'William, what in the world –' She took in the sight of her husband in wet stockinged feet, his face set pale and hard, and she stepped back to let him pass into the house.

'William, whatever ails you today? Look, won't you just –'

'*What?* Won't I just *what?*'

His eyes, the colour of flint and every bit as soft and yielding, glared at her, formidably cold. The quiet, biting control of his voice bewildered her.

'Oh, nothing! Walk through the mire in your socks, why don't you? Just drop the wood in the basket and go! But your boots are sodden and so are your socks – what will you wear to go and retrieve your clogs?'

In William's path to the fireplace, Madeleine had left a stool standing. His hands full of sticks, he kicked it to move it out of his way. As it toppled and fell, Madeleine's cry of sorrow as she saw what was coming preceded by an instant the crash of breaking crockery as the seat of the stool hit the breadbowl on the hearthstone, the beautiful bowl John had given them and Brother Thaddeus had made.

'You *stupid* blasted clumsy idiot!' Madeleine yelled at her husband, who stood frozen, the sticks still held in his hands, unable to bear or believe what he had done.

Beside herself with anger and grief, she pulled the linen cap off her head and threw it to the ground in a gesture of despair as he walked with absolute quietness and control to the fireside, dropped the sticks into the basket, and knelt on one knee by the hearthstone to lift the dough from the broken bowl.

'Leave it!' Madeleine screamed at him. 'Leave it alone! Don't touch it! God alone knows what more damage you'll manage to do. You seem to bring the kiss of death to everything. Just leave it be!'

Very slowly, his face white, William stood up and turned to face her. He looked at her, his gaze appraising and cold, his voice still quiet and perfectly controlled.

'"Witch" doesn't meet the case – I'd have said "bitch" would be better!'

As Madeleine stepped up close to him, he would under normal circumstances have admired the magnificence of her hair tumbling out of its fastenings, and the flash of fire in her eyes. This day he didn't care what she looked like; he was just furious at himself and at her and at everything.

Without stopping to think, incandescent with rage, she lifted her hand to slap his face, but he was quicker, and she found her wrist seized and held with a grip like steel.

'Don't do that,' he said, his voice icy.

'Well, you deserve it!' she bawled at him. 'You *deserve* it!'

'I don't care.' This was a simple sentence, and its import should have been easy enough to grasp. But it took Madeleine a few seconds' pause to pick those three words clear of all the expletives and profanities that came with them. She was not high-born, and in the course of her work as a healer she had mixed with some vulgar folk; but she had never in her life heard such a gross stream of obscenity as William, his voice low and cold and focused, levelled at her then.

He released her wrist and, in his wet socks, walked quietly past her to let himself out of the house. She burst into tears. Weeping, she knelt and lifted blindly the dough in its cloth from the bowl, carried it to the table to deal with later, then picked up the shattered pieces of pottery, and stood with them, heartsick, her tears falling on them. After a moment's indecision, she carried them up to their chamber and laid them on the bed. She took a kerchief from the store of linen in her chest, and swaddled the forlorn and useless heap of broken shards in its soft folds. She buried the bundle beneath her clothes, right at the bottom of the chest. The idea of parting from that gift felt unbearable. It was meant to be forever. She closed the lid of the chest and sank down on the floor beside it, sobbing inconsolably.

She had no idea how long she stayed there, grieving. Her imagination could frame no way forward. But eventually she wiped her eyes and blew her nose on her apron. The dough would be ready. Life had to go on. She went downstairs again, unwrapped the bread sponge from its cloth and picked out two fragments of pottery that had got past the linen to the dough, then kneaded it again for a minute or two, shaped the loaf, and left it to prove while she tended to the oven, lighting another bundle of sticks and hoarded brushwood to bring it up to full heat. She waited patiently until the time and temperature were right, raked the ashes aside and pushed in the dough, sealing up the gaps with flour and water paste as she set the stone in the aperture.

She scrubbed down the table and washed her hands, set the fallen stool on its feet again, under the table this time. Finally, reluctantly, she faced the fact that she'd better go and make peace with her husband. Underneath her sense of injustice and indignation and outrage, she knew he hadn't meant to break the bowl. She knew how much he loved the place of its making and the man whose gift it was.

Madeleine pushed her feet into her clogs and went in search of her man. She wondered if he was still angry with her, and if intrusion would still be unwelcome.

Though the days continued cold, especially in the wind, the air held a promise of spring. It was wet underfoot everywhere, and the twigs of trees and herbs still stood stark and bare in the sunshine, but in the living boughs the bark shone red now, not dull black or sere dun, and Madeleine could feel the rising of life, the turning of the year towards the light. There was hope in the air, and it hummed its healing song in her soul. She went down the path and looked for William in the woodshed, where she saw the flung log with its buried axe-head and the broken haft, and shook her head in wondering disapproval. She looked in the stable, which she found empty – then she saw he had taken the palfrey and tethered her outside.

Eventually she found him, in the barn where they stored the straw and some of the implements they used around their holding. He had been setting new teeth in the rake, replacing the damaged and missing ones. She saw that he had taken off his hood and thrown it across the barn. It lay on the floor near the doorway. She knew why that was. Sometimes, especially when he felt upset or under stress, he could not tolerate anything tight around his throat – around the place where once a rope had tightened when, in utter despair, two years ago he'd tried to hang himself. She bent and picked up the hood.

He had heard her clogs on the stones set into the track and straightened up from the bench against the wall where he had been working, the rake in his hand, turning to face her as she stood in the doorway and looked in.

He did not speak. In the pale, bright February sunshine she saw his face still set grim and bleak. She wondered what to say to him. Evidently he intended to say nothing at all to her. She supposed he must still be angry with her, then.

'Love… ' she said at last, 'love is not a matter of endearments murmured in the bedroom and forgotten in the day's work around the yard. Love is for the everyday, and its courtesies are for the ordinary round, not just for the conquest of seduction.'

She sounded bolder than she felt. The clear challenge of her voice showed him no sign of the odd quailing weakness in her belly. She did not like to admit it, but she had felt afraid of him when he grabbed her arm and swore at her. His face had been possessed of so fierce an intensity, with not a glimmer of kindness anywhere – just cruel, cold fury in his eyes. She was not sure what his reaction to this might be. The prospect of another wave of anger like the last one frightened her. But she stood, chin up, feet planted, and looked him in the eye. He remained quite immobile for a moment, the rake held in his hand. Then he placed it with precision against a frame-joint where it could not slide and fall. The deliberate stillness about him scared her even more. It felt somehow threatening. Such self-control filled her with foreboding. She wondered if he might even hit her. He turned to face her, and the sun from the open doorway behind her shone into his eyes. He squinted to see her, then raised his hand to shield his gaze from the sun. She saw that his mouth was being repeatedly dragged sideways now, by a tic that had started up in his face. The effect was ominous. Even so, she stood her ground. She clutched the hood she had picked up, her grip tightening in fear.

'I know,' he said simply, in reply to what she had said. He took a step towards her. 'Madeleine, I can't see you properly; the sun's in my eyes. I can't see what you're thinking. Are you still angry with me? If I… may I… will it be acceptable to you if I hold you in my arms?'

This struck Madeleine as a very strange question for a man to ask his wife. She was learning that a childhood with no playmates and no affection, followed by three decades in a monastery, had left her husband without any easy instinct for family relationship. Her heart still pounded erratically at the outburst of anger she had imagined. Suddenly she felt quite drained and spent.

'For goodness' sake!' She hadn't meant it to come out sounding so peevish.

She closed the gap between them, and put her arms close around him. She expected him to speak to her, say sorry, explain himself, but he lowered his head onto her shoulder, pressed his face against her neck, held her to him tightly, saying nothing. They stood like that for a long time.

Eventually she stepped back a little from his embrace, and lifted her hands to cup his face, her eyes searching his. Vulnerable, open, he let her look at him, her face still blotched and her eyes red and swollen from weeping over the calamity of the bread bowl.

'I feel so ashamed,' he whispered. 'I feel so guilty. I... can you... will you... forgive me? For the bowl and the hens, and for swearing at you... and I think I might have hurt you too – hurt your arm. Please... it's unbearable... I just need you to forgive me; I can't bear it otherwise, can't bear what I've done.'

Madeleine wondered if the day would ever dawn when she finally felt she'd understood her husband. She thought probably not. So she kissed him instead, and that seemed to go well.

'It's all right,' she consoled him. 'It was an accident.'

Chapter Two

Woken by his incoherent cries, groggy with sleep, only half aware of anything, Madeleine groped under the blankets to make some kind of reassuring contact with her gasping, twitching husband. He sounded afraid. Tangled in another bad dream. She judged it not far off dawn by the smell of the air and the direction of the moonlight, but she certainly didn't feel ready for the morning just yet.

She turned toward him, putting her arm around him, raising herself to kiss his forehead. 'Hush,' she murmured patiently, barely awake herself. 'Hush, my love. Come now, wake up. It's all right. Wake up. Come on. William. Wake up.'

Sudden and startling, his eyes opened and she looked into their dazed and frightened depths of darkness. 'William, it's me – Madeleine.'

One more breath sucked in, shuddering and terrified, then calm gradually returned. She could still feel his heart pounding, though. She lay back in the warm nest moulded to her body alongside him, wondering how he might receive it if she asked what the dream had been. This happened often. He turned aside all probing, saying either that he couldn't remember or that he didn't want to.

He rolled over to face her.

'Will you hold me?' His voice shook, sounding as pathetic as a lost child. She opened her arms and he crept into the refuge of her embrace.

'William, you're trembling,' she said, cradling him to her. 'Whatever was it? What are these nightmares about? Is it from that fire you were caught in at St Dunstan's, or the men who attacked you? What?'

She felt the tension of his hesitation, the breathing in to speak, then letting it go, then breathing in again, and he finally mumbled: 'It was just a memory. Sometimes they come back.'

'Of?' she prompted, and he burrowed in closer.

'My father.' The words blurred indistinct against her neck, and she pulled back a little so she could see and hear him, which he resisted, clinging to her.

'Tell me,' she prompted, her voice soothing and kind, as if she spoke to a small child. Something in her wondered if that was indeed what she was speaking to.

She waited a long time while he brought the words up from some locked place in his soul, and dragged them reluctant into the dim half-light of the dawn. Even that felt like too much exposure.

'I was about... about fourteen I think, and I can't for the life of me remember what insolence of mine had roused him so. It... it never had to be much... just the look on my face... the wrong tone of voice... anything. There was just something about me that drove him crazy at times. He'd be bellowing at me to take that brazen look off my face, but I never knew... I mean I hadn't realized... well, anyway...I remember only standing in the sunlight with the open door behind me, and his face turning dark red with rage as he rose from his seat at the table. I turned to run, but my mother had come in behind, and she grabbed me for him. I tried to struggle free, and I wish I'd fought harder. He took hold of my hair and wrenched me round to face him. He'd unbuckled his belt while I was struggling to get free of my mother's grip, and he held it dangling in his other hand as he yanked my head back and roared in my face: "You saucy, impudent knave! By the time I've finished with you, you'll not want to speak at all!"

'I knew it would be true... It was... By the time he'd done I was nothing but a trodden clot of seeping welts, lying half-conscious in a puddle of my own urine... and all I wanted was to get out of my body somehow, get out of my life, find a way to escape it... Then in the end I did. I got free of them. But it follows me sometimes, comes back to stalk my dreams.'

Madeleine stroked his hair, making room in her soul for the awfulness, wondering if there was nothing human nature would not stoop to. His trembling had almost stopped.

'That's why...' he said then, 'that's why I couldn't have you slap my face when I was so rude to you yesterday. I know how insulting it was, what I said – I know it. I did fully deserve to have my face slapped – but I can't permit it. It just makes me see red. I've had enough of it. I know I'm obnoxious and offensive and all of that, and I realize how nasty I can be... and when I think back on it after, I'm always ashamed of myself. But I... I *cannot* allow you to raise a hand against me, because I just won't have that any more. If you...' He moved his head against her shoulder, nuzzling his face into her warmth. When he spoke again his voice was so muffled she had to strain to make out his words. 'If you could manage to be patient with me when I speak so rude and hurtful, I'll see it for myself and apologize when I can get myself to it.' He turned his face a little and his words came low but clearer. 'I'm sorry now, Madeleine, sorry that I ever had anything to say so spiteful and unfair that you wanted to slap me. I'm truly sorry. It's no wonder you flared up at me. Can you... have you forgiven me?'

'Forgiven you "witch" or "bitch"?' The recollection still stung. He had apologized more than once, and Madeleine felt she ought to be able to leave it alone now, but she found the injury hurt still as she uncovered it. She knew it didn't help to rub his nose in the recollection of what he'd said, and she felt guilty not to capitulate more generously in the wake of the nightmares that harrowed his sleep; but the hit still felt sore.

He lay silent for a few moments. She wondered if this would be the start of another row.

'I know,' he mumbled. 'I know. It's just how I am. You aren't the only person who found me too offensive to bear. I don't know what to do except say I'm sorry. I can't see any way to set it right. Please, Madeleine.'

'Did you not mean it, then – what you said?'

Again he was silent. 'There is nothing good in this,' he eventually whispered. 'I'm begging you to let it go.'

'Oh. So you did mean it.'

'Madeleine… please… well, all right then, yes I meant it. But I'm still sorry I said it. It didn't help.'

She took a deep breath. 'Well then, here's the thing. It still feels bad that you could say that or think it, but when I look back on what passed between us, I have to admit it – you had some cause. And I think I can put up with the occasional laceration to my soul if you can live with my ugly temper and my unsubmissive spirit. I don't expect to be a wife a man could be proud of anytime soon. What I'm saying is, I'm sorry too.'

He lifted his face to look at her, raised himself up on his elbow, brought his hand to her cheek, let his fingertips stray to trace her hairline, her eyebrows, her lips. Serious and tender, his gaze took in every feature, adoring her.

'I *am* proud of you. I… um, I'm not sure it's morally improving to your character to admit this, but I just worship the ground you walk on.'

Softly, he kissed her cheek. 'Madeleine… look… I haven't washed, or rinsed my teeth, and I'm all frowsty from a night's sleep. But if you don't mind it, I believe there's a God-given way to bring back some of the tenderness we let ourselves lose so casually. Will you have me, my lady? Do you want me?'

In the slow grey rising of dawn, the mystery of her dark eyes met his questioning gaze. She saw something teasing, something trusting, but also a shaky thread of uncertainty. He would never be quite sure, she thought; never know without a doubt that life would receive him or that love would be unconditional. Even now, the uncertainty was increasing and his confidence that she would welcome him diminishing. She looked up at him, and as his eyes searched hers he saw a sly shaft of utter mischief come slanting there. A tiny smile brought the familiar dimple to the side of her mouth. Unsure what was happening, or what she might be thinking, he was taken by surprise and was easy to topple when with a sudden, vigorous movement she twisted up and round and pushed him onto his back on the bed, straddling him and glaring down in pretended stern severity in the semi-darkness. Startled and laughing, he looked up at the forbidding dominatrix who had overpowered him. Leaning forward, her river of greying hair surrounding his face, she grabbed his wrists and pinned them back to the pillow.

'Tha'rt a bad lad, William de Bulmer!' She frowned ferociously down at him, the old broad country speech adding coarse sand to the scolding. 'Tha's been a bad lad all thy life! Tha came through thirty years in a monastery unscathed, and nothing I can do or say has taught thee better manners either! Tha'rt a reprobate! A villain! A rascal! Just wait and see what I'm about to do to thee for thy sins!' Her eyes flashed and sparked as she contemplated him trapped on the bed beneath her.

'Oh, heaven, pity!' he whimpered in mock terror. 'Oh Jesu, help!'

For a moment those words gripped Madeleine's heart as she wondered fleetingly how often he had said them in earnest, even as a little child. But she gave no room in her heart to that knife of sadness: she set herself to lifting all the shadows that still haunted him from the bad dreams of his sleep and the nightmares he had lived through waking.

'Nay!' With a savage growl she shook him. 'No help for thee! Tha'rt bad through and through! I'll give thee "witch" and "bitch"! I'll give thee "tu-whit tu-whoo"!'

Genuine bewilderment passed through his mind for an instant. *Tu-whit tu-whoo? What?* And then he remembered how he had scared her in the darkness of the lane as she walked home. He hadn't realized that was still festering away under the surface as well.

He cringed melodramatically. 'Never contradict the enemy when she's got things wrong,' he whined. 'O, I confess I am a bad lad! I am! I always have been! My mouth is bad. My heart is bad.'

She bent and kissed his mouth, his breast – loud, smacking kisses. 'There!' she pronounced. 'Cured! Any other part of you bad?'

'Well…'

She fixed him with a stern look, and then he closed his eyes as the soft, rough cloud of her hair drifted sensuous, human, warm, down his face, his throat, his breast; and he caught his breath in sudden sharp intake.

Madeleine had spent her life collecting arts of healing. It gave her a profound sense of satisfaction to have discovered that whatever else making love may be, it is also good medicine. She chased the terrors that stalk by night clean out of his head.

The sun mounted the horizon in a heady glory of gold and lavender and rose unappreciated and unnoticed by either of them.

'My sweet, my lady love,' he murmured into the tumble of her hair against his cheek, ''tis well daylight. Those hens will be trying to kick their way out, and Marigold will be restless too, for all she's nearly dry. 'Tis long past time we arose.'

They lay one moment longer, reluctant to leave the snug warmth of their bed for the raw chill of the February morning, no matter how bright the sun. William ventured out first, and scrambled into his clothes. He thought he'd wash at some point but, having briefly contemplated the prospect of walking naked down the stairs to draw some icy water from the well, he dismissed it with no protracted inner debate.

So he stood, one foot on the stool as he tied his boots, and glanced across to Madeleine as she stood lacing her kirtle, for she said, ruefully: 'I'm getting fat, William. I eat more in the cold, and you do most of our fetching and carrying. I've cut none of the firewood this winter, you've done it all. You look something less like a skeleton, which is a blessing I'm sure – but I shall be straining the seams of my clothing. I know I'm no little lass any more, but I like to keep trim. Else your fancy might stray elsewhere.'

'Not a bit of it,' he responded firmly. 'Even when you get as fat as Lily the pig you'll be the only woman for me. I love all of you – every yard of you, every ton of you!'

He caught the pillow she threw at him, fortuitously, for it would have knocked the candlestick and mug of water clear off the bedside table, and landed all in the chamber pot.

'Impudent rascal!' she scolded in feigned indignation.

'Aye, right,' he said, tossing the pillow back onto the bed. 'I thought we established that.'

He came round the bed to where she stood now brushing her hair.

'This was my dream,' he whispered, taking her into his arms again. 'This was the thing I imagined, and clung to, all last summer. That somehow, one day, I would be there with you, to watch your hair hang down as you brushed it in the morning. Oh, you play havoc with all of me. "Bitch" I take back. "Witch", I'm not so sure. You've bewitched me!'

She took him by surprise then, pushing him away from her and suddenly stamping her foot.

'Stop it! Just stop it, William! I'm not a witch! I am *not*!'

It was only then that it properly sank in: she really did hate it, it really upset her. She could not bear the idea of being dubbed a witch; and it frightened her too. Absorbing the exasperation and distress with which she beheld him, he recognized that he had held too lightly what it must have felt like to find herself the focus of the mob looking for something to hunt, something to burn, something to tear apart. It had all gone too deep to be chased away by laughing at it.

He nodded. 'No. I'm sorry. You are not. Of course you're not.'

She broke the gaze that linked them and went back to brushing her hair. He paused one awkward moment, then thought it better just to leave things as they lay. He turned from her, and trod light down the stairs to rekindle the embers on the hearth for making their porridge.

As he went from place to place, glad of the spring sunshine and the gradual drying up of the ground, methodically carrying out the chores that shaped the morning, William wondered if in anybody's life peace and understanding could be simply taken for granted. If there were families without touchy people, where no one took offence at an inferred tone of voice or an ill-judged, hasty remark. He supposed not. Presumably in such families there would never be hasty and ill-judged remarks to give offence in the first place; but then – surely – doesn't everyone make mistakes?

He fed Marigold and milked the small amount still to be taken, left her in her stall pulling at fresh hay until the sun should have had a chance to warm the world a little – it was cold, early, to be staking her out with no browsing worth having now, just the fresh air. He took the hens their mash of old bread and hot water and scraps, fed Lily, scratching behind her ears with a stick in the places she couldn't reach, then turned her out as usual. He tended to the needs of his horse; and in the intimacy of the stable, breathing the warm, living scents of straw and good hay and fresh dung, he put his arms around the neck of his palfrey, who stood stolidly munching, moving her ears in interested response as she felt the drawing on her inner resources of human need. 'Nightmare,' he whispered, 'I'm a travesty of a man. I don't do life well.'

She shifted her weight, blowing, and shook her head. The mouthful of hay had all gone and she wanted another. He released his hold on her, bending down to lift the water bucket from its metal frame. He took it to the well.

Walking back to the house carrying empty feed buckets and the can with its precious cupful of milk, William reflected on the immediacy and simplicity of animals, and acknowledged that he found their company less confusing and dangerous than that of humankind.

He left the buckets to be swilled out, set the can with the milk on the scullery table, and came through to take his seat opposite his wife, who had ladled out their porridge in steaming bowlfuls. The morning was cold, and he ate the food gratefully. Madeleine had started hers already, and finished ahead of him. Her eyes rested thoughtfully on her husband.

'You have fine, slender hands,' she observed. He took in this remark, and nothing in the words but something indefinably subtly there in her tone tensed him against attack. He persevered with his breakfast, taking refuge in the last mouthful and wondering what was coming next.

She reached across the scrubbed boards of their table, between breadcrumbs from last night and the empty porridge bowls, and took his hand, tracing his fingers, turning it over. He let her do it, but wariness crept into every corner of him. He sat still, waiting. He thought they should take care to leave no crumbs on the table when they went to bed at night, because it encouraged the mice, but stowed that away for a diplomatic moment to mention it, when he might raise it tactfully, lest Madeleine feel he implied unintended criticism of her housekeeping. For the moment she seemed to have her mind on something, but he couldn't imagine what it might be. She traced with her forefinger the raised blue veins on the back of his right hand.

'Brother Thomas's hands were not like yours,' she mused. 'He had broad, red hands – farmer's hands I suppose... telling a story of working with wood and stone... digging the garden... ploughing the field... mending the barn... What did these hands do – your hands? I think you told me you were no great scholar, so they were not occupied with books of philosophy and theology... and I think you said you had no true vocation as a monk... so I can't see these hands folded quiet in prayer... and I don't remember you saying you had a gift for illumination... I think you might have thought the work of a scribe beneath you... What occupied these clever, slender hands? Money, I suppose... they must have filled their days counting in rents from tenants, paying out when they must for work done... writing in the ledgers... money hands...'

'Money is not such a bad thing,' said William quietly.

'Nay, indeed! Did I say it was?' She withdrew her hand from his.

'You did not.' He raised his eyes to look at her, and the coolness of their disquieting gaze was lowering in temperature every second. 'But I have been listening to contempt my whole life long, and by this time I know it when I hear it.'

She waited a moment, but he lowered his eyes and said no more, and with an air of impatience she reached across and began to collect together their bowls and spoons and mugs, saying nothing.

'Have you done punishing me, then? Or should I be braced for more?'

'Punishing you? What are you talking about?' She stared at him in astonishment.

The long, fine fingers of the money hands played absently with the scattering of crumbs on the table as their owner chose his words with care. Though he did not fear it, neither did he wish to provoke his wife's quick temper.

'I think you are still angry at me for my ill-judged teasing you, calling you "witch". I had not comprehended how deep it went.'

She put the bowls down with a thump, and glared at him across the table, her eyes sparking and flashing. 'How can you say so? How could you fail to see? What kind of idiot are you? They burned my house, they killed my mother, they violated me – all because they said I was a witch! And, William –' her face flushed crimson then – '*I AM NO WITCH!!!*'

He nodded. He lifted his eyes to meet hers. The odd flicker she saw there and took for hostility was no more than reluctance to meet the fury of her stare.

'I know it,' he said softly. 'I never thought you were. I'd hoped to draw the sting of what they did by mocking it.'

'No!' she cried sharp and angry. 'That isn't true! When you said, "I don't know about witch but bitch seems to fit," you were *not* mocking it! You were using it to hurt me!'

He drew a deep breath. 'Yes. Yes, I was. And I am sorry for it, and I've asked your forgiveness for it. And then this morning what I said just before we came down for breakfast... well, I judged it wrong. I didn't mean to hurt you then. I hadn't properly got on board that even when it isn't meant to sting, it does. And on my honour, Madeleine, I will not say it again.'

'Your honour?' She laughed, shortly. 'Oh, well I can rest easy if your honour is the guarantee!'

He looked at her. She could feel him weighing the situation, whether this was worth a full-on slanging match or whether he would let it go, or whatever to reply to the scorn with which she dismissed him.

'Why do you say that?' he asked softly.

During the months she had lived within the abbey close at Peartree Cottage, chatting with Brother Martin the porter, piecing together Brother Tom's cheerful jests with other scraps of passing gossip and remarks that William himself let fall, Madeleine had formed a clear enough picture of his history and the regard in which he had been held. He had told her in sketchy outline about the fire from which he had fled at St Dunstan's Priory where he had been prior; and told her something of the slamming of every door in his face as he sought refuge, until he had begged sanctuary at St Alcuin's. He was never very forthcoming in sharing his memories, but she had been able to make out an accurate working outline of his life.

'Honour, I think,' she pressed on obdurately, 'has not been your strongest suit.'

His eyes are the colour of bright steel, she thought, *and just as hospitable.*

'Well, no; it has not. Then I can offer you no reassurance at all. You will just have to take your chances.'

With a small, deliberate movement, he used his thumbnail to crack in half a fragment of hard breadcrust that lay on the table.

'I have no clear understanding of what attracted you to me, Madeleine,' he said quietly. 'You have not told me. But often enough this year you have told me I am a dolt, an idiot, stupid, a bonehead, a simpleton, a clumsy fool. You tell me now that my honour is nothing. No doubt you are right in every count. What is it, then, fundamentally, the regard of a wife for her man? Is it only affectionate contempt? And if I were to dig deeper to the flinty stuff it's built on, would I find only contempt by itself and no affection?'

She drew breath to reply, and his fingers twitched in an irritable interruptive gesture. He had not finished.

'As a householder, in many ways – not all – I make myself look stupid. I warned you this would be so. I have no grounding in the skills Brother Thomas had that you admired, and that would have served me well here. But I am doing my best, and what more can I do? You knew this when we took our way together.

'As for my hands and the handling of money – assuredly, yes. Without money we were not able to make a life together. The lack of it stood in our way. Money, inherited money, has given us this home, along with our furniture, our chickens, our pig, the hay for the horse and the goat, the straw for their bedding, the hams hanging from the rafters until we've had time to breed our own pigs. Money corrupts, but it blesses as well. It creates stability, and security, both good things. I have handled it in its corruption, and in my own – but I hope I have sometimes handled it to build something worthwhile.

'As to how I became a monk – well, I'll tell you about it if you care to hear it.

'And my honour? Yes, you're right. A vain thing, mostly the figment of my imagination. Not worth mentioning. Not worth anything. I admit it freely. But I still promise you I shall never call you "witch" again; and I hope you can believe me.

'Oh – and I'm sorry I'm not Brother Thomas, but I don't think you'd have found him the easiest man to get on with either, if you'd actually set about the task of living with him.'

With a scrape of his chair on the stone flags of the floor, the unexpected harsh noise of it startling her, he got to his feet then.

'I'll get the wood in. And I think, while the weather's cold and it keeps the stink in check, I'll dig out the night soil from the gong, so if you feel the need to relieve yourself, have pity, won't you? And it's market day. I promised I'd go for some things, if you have a list.'

'Is that it?' she cried after him as he picked up the crockery and carried it through to the sink. 'Is a woman's word not worth waiting for?'

He stopped. The sudden grin that lit his face as he turned back to her took her completely by surprise. 'Good alliteration!' he said.

She stared at him blankly. 'What?'

'Aye, and that.'

'William, will you –'

Now he was laughing. He left the bowls and came back to the table, sat down opposite her again.

'Well, O wise one? What word will work as a weapon to wield to win this William into ways worthier than those in which his wickedness is wont to wend?'

She stared at him. 'You're impossible! You're just impossible!'

'What?' he said. 'Why?' He shook his head, laughing, reaching his hand across the table to her. 'You can have your say! For sure you can have your say. But first, dearest, will you hear this?' His gaze met hers, serious again. 'You and I, we have struck sparks against each other from the very first meeting. I liked the challenge of it – it amused me. And I still… well… I love your spirit, I love the bite of your wit. I love that you see through me and flick aside my every pretension. "Honour has not been your strongest suit," aye, indeed! You don't let me get away with anything. I don't always enjoy it while it's happening to me, but I love you for it.

'But your contempt wears me down, makes me less of a man. It diminishes me. When you call me a fool and an idiot, when you sneer at the occupation of my hands, I hate that. I have to reach deep within myself to try and remember that whatever the world thinks of me and whatever you think, Christ does not hold me in contempt. He may not respect my choices or admire my character, but he accepts me. He does not scorn me. I hold on to that when it feels as though everything else is slipping, and I am losing all sense of myself as ever being able to be worth anything to anyone. I have to reach way down inside to find that hope to hold on to.

'And this ceaseless bickering wears me down. It's carping; it's not wit, it's not fun. When I cross the threshold of our home, for mercy's sake, this should feel like a sanctuary. I should not be bracing myself for whatever might hit me this time – what reprimand, what fault exposed. As I open the door, I take a quick glance at your face to see if I must expect trouble. Sometimes all is well. Sometimes my heart sinks and I think, oh save us, what have I done wrong now? Heaven knows I'm familiar enough with that kind of home: but I've always cherished a dream it doesn't have to be this way. I'm sick of it, Madeleine. I hate it. We are little more than a year married, and I hate it already. This is rougher than playing. I'm always having to defend myself against you... and I can't, not really. You get through all my defences. Every spear you throw finds the softest place in my belly and goes right in. Can't we call a truce? Can't we be friends, you and I, as well as lovers? I know what I am, all too well; might you be willing to be kind to me, and overlook some of it in mercy? God knows I need it! And I'm sorry, for I said I would let you speak and all I've done is go on even more myself. I'll shut up now.'

He kept his fingers entwined with hers across the table, and his eyes held hers briefly, then he looked down, and just waited. Madeleine did not move either, overwhelmed by the torrent of words and hardly knowing what to pick up of all that he had said. The silence between them grew less comfortable as every moment passed. Still he waited.

'I hardly know what to say,' she responded in the end. 'I had thought we were happy together. I can see we have a way to go before we finally shake down comfortably as man and wife, and know each other's ways – but we were old to begin it, weren't we? I didn't know you hated being married to me. I didn't know you thought me unkind, or that you dread coming home. I'm sorry about that. And I certainly didn't intend you to think I was comparing you unfavourably with Brother Thomas. Do you regret it, then – that you married me?'

He looked steadily into the bright challenge of her gaze. 'I do not. I bless the day I married you. Now, then: what did you want to say to me?'

'Oh…' She shook her head. 'It doesn't matter. It'll keep. We've sat here too long talking and there's too much to be done. The days are short. It can wait until we sit down for a bite later on. Be off with you! And thank you for digging out the muck, William – it's not a job you can have been looking forward to. And I must go and see if either of those birds has laid – I need an extra egg for what I wanted to make us for our dinner. There's only one every other day at the moment, but we may be in luck. The morning's running away with us. Let's talk later.'

William hesitated, uncertain about this, feeling that he had said too much and left too little space for Madeleine. He suspected that if he said so, it might seed another argument. So he nodded in acceptance of what she said, and turned to the work awaiting his attention.

As he carried and stacked wood, and sweated over the labour of digging out the heap of night soil that fell from the longdrop closet built out from their chamber, William turned over in his mind the antagonisms of the morning. The time after they had woken and before they got up to see to the animals, the time they met up to eat at midday, and the evenings when they sat together at the fireside were their occasions for conversation. Through the mornings and afternoons of the day they were often engaged on separate chores – or, if they were working together, so fully involved with the task in hand that it occupied their minds completely. In monastic life, the Grand Silence extended past the community breaking its fast, and meals were taken in silence, listening to the reading of the martyrology. All the naturally arising domestic opportunities for conversation blocked. He reflected ruefully that Benedict of Nursia certainly understood about the propensity of human beings for falling out with one another. The only way to prevent it was to stop them talking altogether, it seemed.

A sudden change in the breeze wafted the stench of human manure into William's face, and he turned aside, retching. This task disgusted him almost beyond bearing. He didn't mind the dung of the goat and the horse, for they fed on hay and leaves, roots and grain, and the smell of what left them was not offensive. But the excrement of meat-fed human beings, and that of the pigs that ate the meat scraps from the human table, turned his stomach over with its putrefaction and hideous rottenness. For a moment he stood quite still, pressing the back of his hand against his mouth, swallowing back the saliva that rose in preparation for vomiting, bringing the instincts of his body back under the control of his mind.

As he took the handcart with its vile but precious load through the herb and vegetable gardens Madeleine had planned and he had dug, mostly bare now in this season when the earth lay banded in winter cold, he supposed he should be grateful that he had somehow evaded this task from the day he entered monastic life – cleaning out the jakes had been a duty reserved exclusively for him through the years of his boyhood.

Though the icy well-water shrivelled his skin and left him gasping at the shock of it against his body, William washed every inch of himself before he went in to eat at the end of the morning.

As well as a compact round loaf still hot from the oven and a tiny cheese from the milk Marigold still produced, Madeleine had made a hearty pease pudding. Tasty with stock from poultry bones, onions fried in grease carefully caught as it dripped from roasting birds, marjoram dried in the long days of summer, and sage and rosemary fresh from the garden, it smelt aromatic and appetizing. William said their grace and sat down thankfully, tired and thirsty as well as hungry. Sometimes they drank well-water, but today Madeleine had served him ale. He made a mental note of this, said nothing but wondered why. They ate for a while in a silence that William's mind probed cautiously.

Madeleine tore some bread off the loaf in the middle of the table and reached for the butter.

'I thought I might go and visit my brother.' She glanced up toward him, her face defensive. A woman did not leave her man to fend for himself, cook his own supper, manage the chores alone. Their homestead gave enough work and more than enough for two pairs of hands.

She took in, with one sharp glance, William's raised eyebrow and cautious nod, and interpreted this as a nascent objection.

'Well, I haven't seen him since the day we were wed. I miss him. I'd not normally have let this long go by without a visit. It's only because I married you. And I'd leave you some cheese made, and some bread baked, and you can cook eggs, can't you? Surely you'd be all right by yourself for just a little while! I can walk if it's that you don't want me to take the horse.'

She looked at her husband, who was observing her patiently.

'How long were you thinking of going?'

'Oh, for heaven's sake! How hard can it be to look after a goat, a pig and a handful of chickens for a day or so? Not long, all right? I only wanted to see Adam!' Scanning his face, she took for disapproval William's momentary frown of bewilderment at the use of her brother's childhood name from the days before he became John, his name in religion. 'I meant no more than two nights! Surely you can –'

'Madeleine…' He spoke quietly and reached across the table to touch her hand. 'Stop. Please stop. Before I married you I would not have believed it possible for anyone to have an argument all by herself without a second person joining in, but it seems it is so.'

'I wasn't arguing! William, you're so unreasonable! That's so unfair! I was simply explaining that –'

'I heard you. My love, I heard you. By all means go and visit John. And it wasn't unreasonable to ask how long you'd be gone – was it? The only stipulation I have is that you promise me you can live with what my best efforts can achieve *when you come back* just as much as when you're planning to go.'

'What's that supposed to mean?'

Her husband looked at her thoughtfully. 'I might forget something vital. I might break something. I might burn something. I might let something die. I cannot swear to it that I will not, though I give you my word I will try my hardest to do everything just as you would wish. You can go if you promise me, on your honour – *your* honour, mark you, not mine, so we're safe there – not to tear me to shreds and feed me to the chickens if you get home to discover I've got something wrong.'

Madeleine stared at him in indignation. 'William, that is *so* mean! You make me sound like a complete shrew!'

William added a small piece of cheese to his plate and spread butter on his bread. His lack of haste to refute this supposition kindled indignation into outrage.

'*What?* I don't nag you – do I? I haven't complained when you've been out all day to the market, or to see the lawyer or wherever, without *me* – have I? I have everything to do here myself, with the days short and all – firewood to chop and the animals to feed and the milking and the eggs to collect; not to mention it's lonely on a dark evening here by myself when you go to York and get back home late – and I haven't grumbled, not once!'

'No,' he said softly, 'you haven't. And yes, by all means, you go. Madeleine, I don't understand why you're so angry with me. You told me you want to go and see John, I said that's fine by me; what's biting you?'

'You said I was a shrew.'

'What? I did not! I said no such thing – *you* said it, not me!'

'Well – you were in no hurry to contradict it.'

He stared at her, shaking his head in disbelief. 'Aye,' he said. 'Amen! Look, just go! I signed up to a marriage, not to a war! The peace will be welcome and overdue. Stay three nights, stay a fortnight, but for pity's sake go!'

Madeleine stared at him, her speechless lips parted, her face flushed. She looked straight into his eyes, hurt to the quick, in silent reproach.

He swore, savage and bitter, and pushed his chair back from the table. She drew breath to speak.

'*Shut up!*' he shouted at her, which made her jump, because William hardly ever raised his voice. 'Don't say anything more! Don't say *anything*!'

Monastic habit dies hard. Madeleine registered it on no conscious level, being too wrapped up in that moment in her own pressing sense of grievance, but if she had thought about it she would have marvelled that he went with quiet step to the door, and opened it to leave with the merest faint click of the latch. He got no further, arrested by his wife's voice, plainly on the verge of tears, quavering: 'I knew it would be like this! I knew you wouldn't want me to go!'

His shoulders sagged, and for a moment he just stood where he was. Then he turned to face her, his expression entirely baffled. He stared at her in wonder, and walked back to the place he had vacated. His hands spread on the board, he leaned on the table, contemplating his beloved with bewilderment.

'Madeleine… what have I ever said that made you think I didn't want you to go and visit your brother? You are an intelligent woman. Did you not hear what I said? What's *wrong* with you?'

'Nothing's wrong with me. Nothing at all!' A tear rolled down her cheek. 'I heard what you *didn't* say.'

He shook his head, reaching out to wipe away the tear, which was swiftly followed by another. 'Oh, my love. For mercy's sake, will you try listening to what I have said and not to what I haven't? Go and see your brother. Who knows but he can talk some sense into you. Stay however long you want to. But please – please, please, please – come home loving me.'

'I do love you!' She fought to keep her voice steady with no success at all. 'I don't know why it's always like this! I don't know!' The last word came out in a wail, and she dropped her face into her hands and began to sob. William walked round the table. He said nothing more, but stroked her hair and cradled her head against him. Had he caused this? Was he to blame? Did he start it and not notice? He had no idea.

☩   ☩   ☩

'I begged admittance to St Dunstan's Priory when I was seventeen.'

By their fireside once the evening came, Madeleine carding wool and William sitting quietly watching the flames after putting the supper things away, she had asked him to tell her something of how he came to monastic life. She trod cautiously, not wanting to arouse all over again the antagonisms of the morning; but she felt that if she could understand him a little better, grasp what motivated him, perhaps they would blunder less easily into the spats that scratched and tore and wearied them both.

'I worked for my father then. He was a spice merchant, and he also dealt in unusual hides. I learned from him about buying and selling, trade routes, assessing the quality of animal skins, seeking out trustworthy suppliers. It stood me in good stead later on.

'But at seventeen, I only knew I was trapped. He paid me no wages, so I had no means to move out of our home, which suited him well – I was a hard grafter, and learned quick. I was useful to him, I think, though he never said so.

'Nothing in our life was happy, but I did like going to Mass at St Dunstan's. The priory church rose up cool and lofty, airy, very pale stone – and we had the most beautiful glass in the windows there. I loved the music of the chant, and watching the smoke of the incense rising through the shafts of sunbeams. Everything seemed so calm and measured and under control. So much of what happened to me had to do with being hot and frightened and panicking. And there was so much ugliness in our house. Faces ugly with anger thrust into my face, and I dared not even look away. Ugly fists and ugly threats. The priory showed me beauty... the music, the silences, the silver chalice, the peaceful statue of the Virgin and child. It became a refuge in my mind.

'Everything came to an end at home when I finally stood up to my father – well, if you can call it that. I evaded him hitting me, that's all. He was in his cups – completely drunk, not just a bit tipsy – and I'd passed my curfew for coming in. Even just thinking back to it, I can see him so clear all these years on: swaying, clutching on to the table, shouting after me, commanding me to give account of myself as I started to climb the stairs. I went back and stood before him – it wasn't a wise thing to disregard his summons – and he raved on at me a while, spittle flying into my face and all the usual insults. And when he was done shouting he raised his hand to hit me. And suddenly I'd had enough. I stepped back, and he lost his balance in lunging at me. He fell over the stool and barked his shin on it. He was just staggering back to his feet and I was just weighing up whether taking refuge in my chamber would be enough or if I had to get out of the house until morning, when my mother caught me such a crack on the side of my head with one of the fire-irons I'm surprised she didn't kill me. It caught me off guard, slewed me right over, knocked me onto the floor. And my father let out a great bellow of laughter, and grabbed it from her, and clubbed every inch of me with it. It was all I could do to stay curled up tight and protect my head so I could take it on my back and my legs and not get my nose broken or my skull split or an eye put out. Eventually he'd had his fun, and kicked me and told me to get out. I did. I walked out of the house – with him shouting after me, because he'd meant for me to go to my bed.

'I spent the night curled up in someone's hay barn, waiting for everything to stop hurting, which it did not. In the morning I went to the priory and begged them to take me in.

'The prior – a lazy, decadent brute, but tolerably cunning – wanted to know what gift my family would give them and I said, none. So he wanted some word of my good character from my father or my employer, and I explained he wouldn't be getting it. I told him I'd been beaten until I could no longer stomach it, and beseeched him to take me. He laughed at me, asked me what made me think I'd not be beaten as a novice at St Dunstan's, pointed out I'd not met his novice master, which was true. But I stuck to it, and in the end, I don't know why, he gave way and said I could give it a try. So they took me in.

'The year until my simple vows I grew familiar with their scourges and their penances, and a thousand petty cruelties and deprivations you can impose to make a man's life a living hell. The year between my simple vows and solemn profession things eased off a wee bit. The day I was professed, besides whatever it was I vowed to Christ, I made a vow to my own soul too. I promised myself that somehow I would climb to the top of that pile until I was in charge, and could determine for myself how things went and all the ways of the house. I promised myself that, when I attained it, we would eat well and sleep peaceful, and there would be nothing but beauty all around us. We would have fine victuals and smooth, fiery wines; we would sleep soft and forget the hair shirts, and the scourges could gather dust under the beds. And, by all the foot-licking and hollow flattery and whatever else had to be done, I got there. And I can't say I never had a man scourged, for sometimes I did, and I can't say we walked a path to be admired, for holy we were not. But I got out of all that ugliness and violence, and I stopped it in our novitiate as well.

'Vocation? When I first met you, Madeleine, you challenged your brother when he expressed misgivings as to whether you had any vocation as a Poor Clare. He thought you were seeking refuge only, and you could not build a life on that. You told him you did have a vocation – a vocation to survive. And when I heard that, I thought it possible that you and I could be friends. We had something in common.

'I freely admit my motives were never pure, but... I don't know... what could I have done? I think they would have killed me.'

He moved out of his chair onto his knees to place more wood on the fire. He stayed kneeling there watching the small flames lick at the dry wood.

'I don't know what to say,' she said to him, after listening to him tell the story in that dry, quiet voice so strangely devoid of self-pity or anger. 'I don't know how you ever survived that hell.'

He brushed the clinging remnants of ash and sawdust and cobweb from his hands. 'Cauterized, I think,' he said, 'at some root place in my soul. Besides which, I believed in something good. I had an irrational, unquenchable hope that I could find my way to something of blessing, something I could believe in. And I had this vision of what a home could be: a hearth of loving kindness, a place of shelter and affirmation... and peace.'

Still on his knees, he turned to face her, and shuffled across to where she sat. She set aside the carders with their rollag of fleece, folding her apron up to cover the debris of moss and seedheads and greasy dust that had fallen into it, so he could curl up against her and lay his head in her lap.

'William, I have a long way to go before I can help you make the kind of home you've dreamed of. I'm too hasty, and too sharp-tongued. I'm not patient and I'm not meek. But, if it helps you to know it, with every breath and every day I live, I love you. I don't even know clearly what it is in you I love. I just feel right with you. When you hold me, I know I've come home. When we unite as man and wife, I feel complete. I can see all too well how I've tried your patience and how long-suffering you've needed to be. And the reason I want to go see my brother is to seek his counsel. There must be a reason they make a man an abbot. I thought he might have wisdom I hadn't taken seriously, thinking of him as only Adam – a loud-mouthed urchin tumbling in the dirt, climbing trees, playing out on the moor. I wondered if he could help me learn how to build a place of peace, the way you dreamed it might be.'

He lifted his head from her lap and kneeled up so he could pull her into his arms.

'Sweetheart, you have heard – please tell me you have – that you go up to St Alcuin's with my blessing; and that I think after a year of day-in day-out learning, this homestead and its birds and beasts will be safe in my care. Maybe when you go, you might take him one of the ram's horns we got in the market after the Martinmas slaughtering – it'll make good toggles for Father James.'

His kiss, lingering and tender, healed something between them, putting in its place peace and understanding. The rest of the evening they talked of plans for the spring – how the vegetable garden might be laid out this year, how many pigs they might run in the orchard, whether they might make a start on keeping sheep if any orphan lambs became available, and maybe look to hatch some goose eggs, think about eating goose at next year's Christmas dinner. As they talked, Madeleine carded the fleece John had sent her, and by the time the fire died down a full basket of rollags stood ready for spinning. William took the lantern round to ensure that all was well with their livestock before he climbed the creaking stairs to their bedchamber where the moon shone in through their window. When they settled down to rest, he kissed his wife, and Madeleine felt of a certainty, held in his arms, that though they still had much to learn in living together, she could trust this love; it would not fail her. Contented and reassured, looking forward to her trip up through the hills to the moors, she drifted off to sleep at her husband's side.

She was half woken by his struggling and thrashing, by broken impotent cries. 'No!' he managed to articulate. 'No! No!' Another bad dream.

'Sssh...' Still dopey, Madeleine reached out to touch him, then was startled into complete wakefulness as he suddenly sat bolt upright in the bed and exclaimed with harsh vehemence: 'I am *not* scum! I am *not*!'

He sat there trembling then, and she clambered up onto her knees beside him, holding him close to her, rocking him, hushing him gently.

'What? What?' he murmured, confused.

'You were dreaming,' she said. 'Lie down.'

She soothed him back to sleep and, once she had satisfied herself that he was settled, drifted down out of consciousness again herself, and slept deeply until morning, when she opened her eyes to find her husband already awake, lying quietly alert, just watching her. This slightly startled her.

'William de Bulmer,' she said, speaking with the candour of a mind not fully woken up, 'you have the scariest eyes of any man alive.'

He wrinkled his nose, and a little frown creased his brow. Puzzled and taken aback he considered her words.

'Scary? What d'you mean?'

'Are you seriously telling me you didn't know this?'

'Well, I… I – how could I? I can't see my own eyes, can I? I've spent thirty years in a monastery. Gazing into my eyes and telling me what impact they made wasn't something anyone did.'

'People weren't scared of you, then?'

'Oh! Yes – certainly they were. I was prior a lot of years – it was my job to scare people.'

'Is that so? Is that how you see the work of a superior?'

'Um… yes. Power, responsibility – you have to make it work. Everyone's out to manipulate you, secure your support for their private plans, annex some of what you bring to further their ambitions. If you intimidate them a little, it buys a breathing space. If you intimidate them a lot then maybe you can even use them to advance your own ambitions. That's how it is.'

Madeleine rolled onto her back, away from him. She wished she hadn't said anything. She wished she'd stayed asleep. 'That sounds… I don't know what… chilling… miserable… It sounds like a world in which no one could possibly flourish or be happy.'

She could still feel the scary eyes watching her.

'No. Well, I wasn't happy.'

She frowned.

'But… have you never thought that it wasn't the scary world you'd fallen into that made you unhappy, but the scariness you brought to it that made it unhappy?'

He rolled back to lie flat beside her on the bed. The space between them was narrow, but it felt to him to be expanding like a tundra. He didn't speak for a while.

'We need to take a broom to those cobwebs in the rafters,' he said then.

She made no reply. The silence widened further. Something she appreciated in William was his ability to bear silence – to let it question and challenge him, make him uncomfortable, examine him. Aware of him allowing the waves of silence to conduct their usual rigorous and merciless inquisition, she wondered briefly if her questions and observations were torturing him. 'Am I bullying you?' she asked him, very simple and direct.

He sighed; not, she thought, in impatience or irritation, but just because whatever was happening was cutting very deep.

'Just going into the middle of me with a ploughshare, I think. The pain's only incidental, not the point of it.'

'Tell me, then: does my brother keep peace at St Alcuin's by scaring people?'

'Yes. To some extent he does and he has to. But he is also loved, and with every good reason – which I was not, for equally good reason. He can be intimidating, and he knows it, and he doesn't hesitate over it. But there is nothing cruel in him, and there is a strong streak of cruelty in my nature. I am not a good man, Madeleine. I have hurt people in my life, and thought nothing of stepping on them for my own ends with no regard at all for what it did to them. Perhaps that's what you can see in my scary eyes.'

'Ah! No!' His honesty moved her, and she admired the courage it took to admit his own shortcomings as frankly as he always did. She lifted herself up to lean on her elbow, looking down at his face, bringing her hand to trace his features, her fingers exploring the ridges and hollows. 'Your eyes are scary because they are light and changeable. It's hard to say what colour they are – green, grey, blue? Who can say? Like the sea, like the sky above the moor when the light is changing. It's almost impossible to know what you're thinking. But at the same time, they aren't vague. Your gaze is as focused as a hunting animal, like a fox or a cat creeping up on its prey. I should think anyone that gaze fell on knew a sudden urge to run.'

He turned his head towards her, and his eyes met hers. *That's what I meant*, she thought, *light and shadow like a storm sky gathering over the hills – what am I seeing? Have I hurt you? Are you angry? Are you sad?*

'Run?' he said. 'Do you want to run from me?'

He brought both hands up to his face suddenly then, pressing his fingers to his temples. 'Oh, for the sake of all that is holy, Madeleine! I have known enough of fear and destruction. Can you not try to understand me? Or if not that, at least accept me as I am… whatever that is…'

He let the heels of his hands sink down to cover his eyes, and kept them there.

'There's work to be done,' he said, his voice dull. 'It's well past daybreak, for all it looks so dark out there this morning. Those poor beasts will be wondering where we are.'

He took his hands from his face and swung up and round to sitting on the edge of the bed in one movement.

'Hey! Wait!' Madeleine scrabbled across the tumbled blankets after him. She knelt behind him on the bed, her arms enfolding him, her hair tumbling soft round his shoulders and his breast.

'You don't make *me* want to run!' she reassured him. '*I'm* not afraid of you.'

'No,' he said. 'No, I can tell. It's of no great moment, my sweet.' He put his hands up to her encircling arms. 'Let me go, then, my love – let's get everything here fettled up and in good order, then mayhap you can take off for the abbey sometime in the next few days, if today's dark clouds come to nothing and the weather stays passably fair.'

He twisted round and kissed her lightly, with the kind of smile that is a gift of love rather than spontaneously arising.

'William,' she said in a small voice, kneeling on the bed still in her shift, watching him as he pulled on his clothes, 'you're not angry with me, are you?'

He shook his head. 'I am not. I've slept badly and spent most of the hours of darkness dodging nightmares. It does me no good to talk of my childhood as we did last night. Those demons are best left in the bowels of hell where they belong. And I'm concerned that once again the sun is well risen with the fire not lit and the oatmeal not soaked, and nothing attended to outside. I'm turning into a sluggard and a lie-abed, and I feel guilty about it. But I'm not angry, not with anyone – and most certainly not with you.'

He reached across and rumpled her hair with a quick smile, and then he was gone.

Chapter Three

Abbot John looked up at the rooks startling into cawing flight from the bare branches of tall trees encircling the burial ground. It occurred to him that the rooks might be watching the brothers too. Same view. A community in black braving the weather.

The clouds massed forbiddingly today, and the wind bit cold.

'Requiem æternam dona ei, Domine, et lux perpetua luceat ei. Requiescat in pace.'

The monks gathered round the grave responded, 'Amen.'

'Anima ejus, et animæ omnium fidelium defunctorum, per misericordiam Dei requiescant in pace.'

'Amen.'

And so they laid Brother Ambrose in the ground, facing east to await the coming of his Lord on the Last Day. It had taken Brother Thomas all of yesterday plus some of the afternoon before to dig the grave, for the earth soaked from rain and snow this hard winter had frozen solid. He'd had to take a pickaxe as well as a shovel. Filling in the grave looked like no task for the faint-hearted, either. Everything was damp all day and nobody could think straight. It felt too cold to pray, too cold to work. The men in the scriptorium and the robing room found their fingers too clumsy for precision. Theodore had the fire banked high in the novitiate after he found one of his novices huddled in his cell weeping with cold, in the semi-dark that prevailed even at midday.

All day long the wind blew off the moor from the north-east, bitter cold. It smote against the brow like a blow and nibbled painfully round the edges of unprotected ears. Anyone breathing through an open mouth, the wind slid straight in like a knife into the throat. Huddled birds crouched pitifully among the bare twigs of shrubs and low trees, waiting for Brother Cormac to throw them bread because the ground was frozen, the seeds and berries all gone from the bushes now.

The abbot gave orders for fires to be kept alight everywhere, and for the men to break their fast with porridge every day, not just bread and water.

'Look out, abbot's on the prowl,' Brother Cedd warned Colin, one of the two new postulants. 'You'll bring trouble on your head if he sees you handling wood without mittens.'

The words had barely left his mouth and Colin was still in the act of straightening up stiffly from bending over the frame he was filling with logs for the infirmary, when Abbot John came round the corner of the wood yard, and stopped, his attention caught.

'Brother, what are you doing? Show me your hands. Look at that, will you? Blotched purple and orange and white – it's too cold. You'll be getting chilblains. That's how they come – when you get your hands and your feet too cold, and then you go back inside – likely as not into the warming room to hold your fingers to the fire because they hurt so from the cold. The sudden alteration is too much. You must take care of your hands. Go back inside and get some mittens. Yes – now! I don't want to see you – *any* of you – working out in this weather with bare hands. Brother Cedd, you should have reminded him. It is a neglect of charity to let him put his health at risk like that. You should be ashamed of yourself.'

He spoke with more severity than he normally would, because he felt anxious and guilty. This was not a good time for his cellarer to die. The extra fires, the extra food – he needed advice to reassure him of the boundaries between necessary charity, advisable leniency, and extravagance that must stop. And a visitation from the new bishop looming later in the spring. He cursed himself that Brother Ambrose's death had caught him on the hop like this. He acknowledged the truth of it was that William had left everything in such good order that, with the bequests from old Mother Cottingham's will just over a year ago, he had felt the constant nagging concern over their financial state lift, and relaxed too much. He knew Brother Ambrose was very old, knew he had to find another cellarer – but none of the men seemed just right for the work, and the easing of the situation allowed him to believe everything could roll along for another year or two. Just as soon as he'd caught up with the pastoral needs of vocational oversight, and improved his skills in the area of biblical exposition, and got to grips with the complexities of the abbey's role as a landlord, and paid some heed to whatever was happening in the school, he could turn his attention again to the task of replacing his cellarer.

And then Brother Ambrose had died; a sudden, quiet, unexceptional death. The old man had slipped out of this world in his sleep, his face peaceful and innocent in repose, wearing his stockings and a shawl tucked around him because the night was cold. When they called him, Abbot John had taken a moment to look with reverence on holy death and commend his brother's soul to God in prayer, twenty minutes to organize the laying out and removal of his body and the thorough cleaning of his cell, and then made himself look steadily at the dilemma he had created in not acting more timely, not finding someone to learn the work while the system ran smoothly and there remained an obedientiary alive to pass on what a cellarer needed to know.

The worst of it was that it made him face up to a further problem he had been avoiding: in Father Chad he had the most awful prior. An abbot needed at his right hand a man of authority and effectiveness, someone with enough confidence in his own judgment to allow humility and decisiveness to co-exist comfortably in his personality. A prior had to be like a rock. There must be no shifting ground in his soul. He must be shrewd, capable, unflappable, likeable, thick-skinned, and have his hand on the pulse of the abbey's life. With a really good prior, the unexpected demise of the cellarer would be an inconvenience but not a disaster. With an insecure ditherer holding the obedience, they had a problem as big as all three ridings of Yorkshire. John felt ashamed and embarrassed that this was compounded by his own unworldliness. He was no aristocrat. He had not been born to ruling men and managing wealth and administering great swathes of farmland and governing the decision-making processes that would affect the lives of scores of tenants in addition to the sons of his house and the various other inhabitants of the abbey's demesne.

Even so, out in the woodyard his conscience pained him like a bit of gravel stuck to the sole of his foot. He shouldn't have spoken to a postulant with such asperity. The young man had looked more frightened than chastened. Abbot John turned back, and followed the mittenless miscreant all the way to the novitiate.

'I'm sorry, Colin,' he said humbly when he caught up with him. 'I didn't mean to speak so sharp. I had something on my mind – felt a bit burdened. But I shouldn't have taken it out on you. You must protect your hands though, in this cold, or they will be damaged – and that's pure misery. That's all I meant.'

And having attended to that, he returned to his own lodging, recognizing that the extent of their predicament was exposed by the fact that he knew he would seek Brother Thomas's advice, simply because from Tom he would hear better sense than he could expect from Father Chad.

'Tom, I don't know what to do,' he admitted. 'The bishop will be here digging into every nook and cranny if all I've heard of him is true. It's imperative we have everything in order. Brother Ambrose was old. I've had a year to prepare myself, and done nothing. I have to confess, I think I may not have the stature of spirit for what I've taken on in this obedience.'

'Nay, neither you nor any man!' Tom responded stoutly. 'That's why we pray. There will be a solution. In this case, if the rumours I've heard are true, it probably lives ten miles to the south-west.'

John stared at him, taken aback. 'You... you think I should seek the help of William de Bulmer? I must admit, it had crossed my mind, but...'

Tom watched his abbot wrestling with his uncertainties as to the propriety of this possibility. 'Look,' he said, 'all you have to do is call on him and ask his advice. If you judge it right to let him loose here again, well you'd stand within your rights to do so; but meanwhile you can slip out quiet-like and just see if he has any helpful guidance to offer, can you not? He may have flown the coop and made his roost in the wilderness, but he's got his head screwed on even if his wings weren't clipped. If you see what I mean.'

'Er... yes, I think so... Well, I'll consider it.'

Abbot John tried without success to attend to other matters awaiting his attention, but his mind was riveted onto this central dilemma of having no cellarer. At this precise minute it posed no grave problem, but once the spring came all that would change. It would be unthinkable to have nobody holding that obedience when the Easter triduum faced them with its influx of guests and pilgrims, and impossible to manage the wave of administration around Lady Day when all the rents were due in. Happily Easter fell late this year, which bought them a little time, though it meant the new bishop's visit would be on them before they had time to catch their breath after the pilgrims had departed. Lent did not begin until the second week of March, and they had not yet seen out January. Ideally he needed to see a new man in place by Candlemas; but it would be unfair – and unrealistic – to expect anybody, however capable, to get a handle on so complex an obedience very quickly, even if he'd had someone primed to step up to the appointment tomorrow. They needed every flying minute of the time they had to get this space filled.

However hard he thought about it, nobody came to mind. He sat frowning, unaware of his fingers drumming the table, mentally searching every face, every personality in his community. Germanus, maybe? Thoughtful man, not greatly occupied. Francis? Or maybe he could kill two birds with one stone and ask Father Chad to take on the cellarer's work, which would dislodge him from his ill-suited role as prior. Would he be any good as a cellarer? Chad was meticulous – fussy even, at times – dedicated, hard-working, dutiful. Not especially imaginative. Mild in his manner. He had been part of the community since forever, which was good. As prior, he had been privy to every decision made in the last two decades or so – except those decisions that William had re-assigned to himself without asking anyone during his brief and eventful stay in their midst. Chad, then? Was it right? *Was* it? John felt paralysed. He could not afford to make a mistake here. And who would stand in as prior?

'Should I ask the community, at Chapter?' he asked aloud. Brother Tom had finished all that needed doing in his abbot's house, but he was lingering, making himself look busy, cleaning things twice, because he had an idea his superior might welcome a listening ear and a second mind on the problem.

In response to this question Tom came, the small brush and shovel for the ashes still in his hands, to stand opposite his abbot, facing him across the cluttered oak table.

'I see where you're coming from,' he said, 'but whatever you decide on this one, I would counsel you to tell them, not ask them. In every community there are men who think a question is an invitation to object. No conversation is nicely rounded off for them without a winner and a loser. Even here. The way I see it, Father, is you don't have too many options. If you put the one solution you have up for grabs and have to sit and watch men evil-tempered with cold and dark tear it to shreds, what will your next proposal be? You haven't got one. It's fair to tell 'em if you mean to bring William back here – but tell them, don't ask. But before you do that, go and see him. He may have better ideas of his own than you or me. I hope I'm not speaking out of turn.'

John stared at Tom in an agony of indecision. Brother Tom waited a moment lest he be further required, then turned away quietly and returned to the careful and meticulous sweeping of hearth and chimney stones.

John sat, twisting his lips between thumb and forefinger, calculating risks and advisabilities, and seeing no new options emerge.

'I'll go and see him,' he concluded finally. 'I just don't know what else to do. Will you ask Brother Peter to get Bess ready? She's not had much exercise through the winter – tell him not to worry, I'm not going far and I won't ride her hard. I'll ask Father Chad to look after the office for me, and set off directly.'

And so it was that, just shy of noon, William, sitting at the table under the window with their household account books working out how much of a dent in their budget the hire of a ploughboy would make, and Madeleine, spinning at the fireside, caught the sharp ring of a horse's shod hooves against the stones in the lane. Both paused in their tasks as they heard the thud of iron on wood that meant the gate latch had flicked over, and realized the rider had turned into their yard. William lifted his head.

'Expecting anyone?'

'Nay – I thought you must be.'

They listened to the silence as the rider dismounted, the metallic thud of the gate latch dropping back into place, and the slow clop of the horse now led across the flagged yard, then both of them abandoned their tasks and went to the door.

'Adam! Adam!' After a brief hiatus of astonishment Madeleine closed the gap between herself and her brother in a racing whirl of skirts and flung her arms around him. 'Oh, how wonderful to see you! And how strange that you came just now – I've been missing you. William and I were only talking about it a day or so back – I've been thinking to make my way up to the abbey for a visit – and now here you are! Oh, I can't tell you how pleased I am to see you again!' As he dropped the pack he had untied, to catch his sister in his embrace, John felt William quietly detach old Bess's reins from his grasp. William led her along to their stable, empty during the hours of daylight, and there unsaddled her, gave her a cursory brush down and half a bucket of water. She was sweating and the well-water was icy cold. He didn't want her to drink too much too fast. He closed the door on her and went for some hay to refill the rack above the manger, bringing a generous armful back from the barn to the stable.

John went into the house with Madeleine, and gave her the gifts he had brought of butter ('Oh, God love you! That's so welcome! Our goat's almost dry, she's kiddling soon') and beeswax candles ('Adam, these smell like heaven!'), then he left her tidying away the things on the table ready to set out a meal for them to share, and went to find William. He rounded the corner of the house, looked and listened, and identified the building that must be the stable.

William, stuffing the net with hay, glanced up and smiled at his friend as John came into the doorway.

'A beard suits you,' John greeted him, returning the smile; 'and that shaggy hair – but it's done nothing whatsoever to disguise your identity – I'd know those eyes anywhere!'

'Well met, Father Abbot,' William replied. 'I've missed you. What brings you here? Trouble? Whatever it is, you are most heartily welcome. As ever, you bring a breath of peace with you.'

Two strands of thought twined together in John's mind then. One was William's question and how he might answer it, the concerns for which he needed William's help. But a second thread tangled itself unobtrusively in with the first – he thought William seemed not entirely happy. Despite the genuine warmth of his welcome, John sensed in him a reserve, a stillness, that he associated with pain. 'Is all well?' he asked, instead of answering William's question.

'Oh,' William replied, patting old Bess, the abbey's sway-backed mare, as he came out into the sunlight to greet his friend, 'we are astonishingly well provided for here. The magnanimity of this gift amazes me every living day. We have a way to go yet to establish ourselves; we have barely made a start in this first year – I am not very handy, as you know. But we have the blessing of an income as well as the house and land; we are bountifully provided for.'

As he talked, he bolted the half-door of the stable behind him, and put a hand lightly on John's back in invitation to accompany him back to the house. John picked through the information William had just given him, searching for something real. 'Was that an answer, or the evasion I think it was?' he asked. But they had reached the house door, and William leaned forward to open it, then stepped back to allow John to precede him inside.

Madeleine stood at the table. She had set out three wooden bowls into which she ladled generous portions of pottage. A loaf of bread, today's baking still warm, sent out an inviting aroma. Two round white cheeses, precious and small, were all that Marigold's yield could now offer. Madeleine had stirred chopped sage into the curds, and the result looked pleasing and appetizing. As the men came in from the yard, she was just adding to the table the butter that John had brought.

'Nothing fancy,' she said apologetically. 'These are lean months. We're drying off the goat and we've little in store.' She glanced at John, then added hastily: 'I mean, we are not short of anything we need, but you know how it is – goes against the grain to buy at the market what we might make shift to provide for ourselves, and will do, given time. Anyway, you're welcome to what we have, and we are not hard up. We can buy what we haven't grown and stored. We should have a second goat soon, in the spring maybe. When William's accounts give us permission. Look, William – butter! From St Alcuin's cows!'

John smiled as William murmured his thanks with real appreciation, but he noted the hint of sarcasm as his sister spoke of William's accounts.

'William's way with accounts is legendary,' he said, as they took their seats at the table; then added quickly, seeing the shadow of wretchedness passing over his friend's face: 'Nay, truly! That was no jest. It's why I'm here. No household goes far without a careful eye on its books, and our Brother Ambrose has died. I've been remiss, I've let the community down. I'd put no one in place to learn the ropes, and now we are without. I've no idea who to ask; and even if I had, I've no one to ease him into all that will be asked of him in that obedience. We might have stumbled along until I thought of something, but the new bishop has chosen us for a Visitation in May, and from all I've heard he's something of a zealot in every respect. They say he's high-minded in his doctrine and more than scrupulous about every facet of administration and propriety of life. I'm not worried about the doctrine, or our life generally – we're in fairly good shape I think. It's the administration where things are shaky under me. I relied completely on Father Ambrose – and on your good work, which he in turn relied on. I don't know what to do, how to get something in place quickly to be sure we have all in order. I took counsel of my esquire, and he encouraged me to come here and beg assistance.'

'Oh,' said William thoughtfully, tearing the bread as he listened to this, and gesturing to John to help himself to a piece. 'It wasn't your prior's counsel you sought, then? Your *esquire*? Will you say grace for us, Father?'

'Well, that would be Brother Thomas, wouldn't it?' asked Madeleine, after they had bowed their heads for the Latin grace and left a moment's pause for reverence. 'What's wrong with that? I'm only hazarding a guess, but I'd have thought you'd get more sense out of Brother Thomas than out of Father Chad.'

'Aye, right, so you would!' William said drily. 'Then why on earth doesn't he get a better prior?'

'Oh, William, don't be so sour!' Madeleine exclaimed. 'And mind your own business!'

John grinned and William shrugged, turning his attention to his pottage. 'I think it's becoming my business, isn't it?' He laid down again the spoon he had lifted. 'Father Chad is who should be stepping in for Brother Ambrose.'

'For goodness' sake!' Madeleine rolled her eyes impatiently. 'There's no need to be such a stickler about status and position! After all, you broke enough rules yourself while you were there.'

A flash of irritation sparked in William's eye. His voice when he spoke was a shade quieter and softer than before. 'In truth, so I did. You haven't understood, Madeleine. I'm not thinking of order and hierarchy. John's prior is there to watch his back, to keep an ear to the ground. If an abbot can't turn to his prior for good counsel when trouble arises, he's more vulnerable than he ought to be. There's nothing wrong at all with Brother Thomas, he's a man of good sense. But it shouldn't be his esquire that John is relying on. That's all.'

'Can I say something?' John smiled at his friend. 'William's entirely right, Madeleine; and he's not picking holes – he cares about my welfare, and I'm grateful. I'm still finding my way, and I haven't got everything sorted out yet. If you can advise me about a prior and about a cellarer I shall be even more in your debt than I already am. But you don't have to put your mind to it this very instant. Your good lady has set some delicious food before you, and I think it's worth appreciating.'

'Thank you!' said Madeleine. 'Come here more often and tell him that!'

William picked up his spoon again and addressed himself to the bowl of stew. John, unconsciously frowning in puzzlement, watched him a moment before beginning his own food. Something seemed amiss here. The subtle fingerpads of his soul were feeling rough edges beneath this conversation.

'Madeleine, this is delicious!' he exclaimed. 'I must indeed come here more often. This is so flavoursome, and the bread is excellent too – just how I like it. Reminds me of home.'

William, silent, felt his stomach slowly contracting in guilt and self-reproach that he rarely thought to compliment his wife on the food she made for him. He thought of adding, 'Yes, it's really good,' but rejected that course of action; it would sound hollow coming from a man who mostly did not think to express his appreciation – as if it had been said for John's benefit not for Madeleine's. The old knot of shame tightened inside him until he felt he couldn't eat another mouthful of anything.

He glanced up, met John's gaze. *What?* John's eyes were asking him. *What's the matter?* He didn't want that question.

'There's plenty more in the pot!' Madeleine's words mercifully saved him from having to think of anything to say. 'And don't hold back on the bread, I can make some more if it's all gone. William, are you not hungry? I never knew a man with so little appetite!'

Now both of them stopped and looked at him.

'Sweetheart, I'm sorry.' William crumbled a morsel of bread and raised his eyes to hers. 'I... listening to John, I just realized how little I bother to tell you how much I enjoy the meals you prepare for us, and how much it means to me... not the food only, but our home here together, and the way you care for me and make everything comfortable.'

He reached across the table, and his fingertips traced a light caress on her work-worn hand. 'Thank you.'

Madeleine smiled. 'William de Bulmer, you are such an oddity! So full of unexpectedness. Have some cheese, my love – you like this cheese.'

That's better, thought John. Knowing William would feel more like eating if that ceased to be the focus of attention, he said: 'So, my friend, help me! Among our brethren at the abbey, who can I possibly find to fill Brother Ambrose's shoes, let alone yours?'

William ate a spoonful of stew – 'You know, this really *is* nice, Madeleine' – and cut a small wedge from the round goat's cheese, adding it to a fragment of bread. 'I do have a suggestion to offer,' he added, glancing at John; 'but I fear it may be a bit controversial…'

'Oh yes,' John answered him, laughing at this, 'and heaven forfend that William de Bulmer should be the one to initiate anything controversial!'

William raised an eyebrow in mock disdain. 'Brother Cormac is who I would choose,' he said.

'Cormac? Oh. Heaven save us! I would never have thought – I can't imagine Cormac anywhere except the kitchen!'

'No? Then it's time you moved him. His cooking's atrocious anyway. I don't see how you all survived it so long. Must be the holiest men on earth. Well, you are – you took me in.'

'We did, and you pulled us into shape admirably in the short time you were with us. I don't think we're about to be crushed under the weight of our own haloes any time soon. But, Cormac – would he not… is he not… well – just a bit abrasive to be dealing with the folk who come and go? He has a good heart, and the brothers esteem him I think, but… he can be… difficult.'

William smiled. 'So I've heard, but I think the legend is an exaggeration. Cormac is discreet, as I have discovered for myself, and he has a generous heart; he's a compassionate man, and it wouldn't do to make anybody cold or unimaginative your cellarer. As for being abrasive, good, bring it on! A cellarer must say "No" at least as often as "Yes", and if people are scared to ask in the first place, all the better. The tradesmen and the tenants are forever trying to cheat you and presuming on your charity: you need a stout heart and a character that no one can intimidate standing at the gate. He's shrewd, nobody's fool; keeps his own counsel; not impressionable. No one can push him around, he does what he thinks is right and it's impossible to budge him. And, which is worth its weight in gold, he's intelligent. You put Brother Thaddeus or Father Chad in that seat and you can start making plans to close down the whole enterprise right now. Cormac's your man. I know he is.'

His gaze, bright and interested, rested on John's face. 'What? Can you not see it?'

'Oh – yes!' John turned the proposal over in his mind, considering. 'The more I think about it, the more sense it makes. It's just that I would never have thought of it myself and I'm getting used to the idea. He isn't going to like it, you know. He's firmly burrowed into his nook in the kitchen. It's where he feels he belongs.'

'Dig him out, then. Good for him.'

John nodded thoughtfully. 'I will. That's a most excellent suggestion. Thank you. I knew you'd know. Will you still come and help us though? Just look over the books for me, and – once I've had chance to ask him – show Cormac what's needed and help him. It's a big favour to ask, I do realize. It might need you to make two or three trips over to us. Can you... would you?'

'Not only is it unlikely that I would refuse you anything, but yes, I'm sure this is an easy thing for me to do. I will come... Of course I'll help you. Only...' he spoke softly, avoiding John's eyes: 'it will be difficult for me to do this without having some conversation with a number of the brothers – your kitcheners and fraterer, your guestmaster, Father James in the robing room, your sacristan, and Father Gilbert and Father Clement – maybe Brother Thaddeus and Brother Stephen too. What do you… what would you feel about that?'

The healer in John saw clearly the hurt in William's sense of exclusion from the community. 'I think I feel I could trust you to take care of this for us,' he said. 'And I think I can trust our brothers in community to understand.'

William nodded. 'All right then. When?' He grinned, as John hesitated, embarrassed. 'Oh, I see – yesterday is hardly soon enough! Well, what does my lady say? If I go back with your brother, I shall be some nights away – as few as possible, but more than one. Is that – can you manage? You may even feel our livestock is in safer hands with me ten miles away!'

His eyes, rueful, looking for reassurance, sought hers. She looked back, her face teasing him, knowing she could shame and embarrass him with the story of the hens. But she did not.

'It sounds as though they need you, my husband,' she replied. 'I'm sure I can manage on my own for a night – or even two or three if they find they can't spare you.'

William still hesitated. 'The only thing is… John, I'd promised Madeleine she might take a few days to come up and visit with you herself. It doesn't seem quite fair… I know you're here now, but… Do you see what I mean?'

'Oh, nonsense, don't mind me!' Madeleine cut in quickly. 'They need you, husband. You must go. We can take turns. I'll go when you come back.'

'Well… if you're sure… It's just… well, it seemed to matter very much…'

She waved his misgivings aside, and William thought it probably best to commit to silence the extent of the importance she had attached to the visit when they had discussed it before, and the tears that had been shed on that occasion. His eyes questioned hers. She nodded, impatiently. Her brother needed him. What more was there to be said?

When they had finished their meal, they left the scraps and plates on the table, wanting to show John their home before he and William had to be on the road – the days were short, the sun began setting in the late afternoon, and no one wanted to be out on the road longer than they must after night folded down.

John rejoiced with them in their spacious homestead. Being daytime, the hens were out foraging, so no explanation was necessary as to why their numbers should be so surprisingly few. He appreciated and affirmed and admired, and delighted in their pride and pleasure in their home. And then, William having fetched a cloak and put together his small necessities in a bag, he and John went out to make ready the horses while Madeleine cleared away the remains of their meal. Suddenly remembering their conversation about her own plans to visit her brother, she ran upstairs to the chest where the curling ram's horn was stored away, that William had suggested she take with her as a gift to the abbey. She brought it down and opened the pack her husband had left ready on the table, tucking the horn in between the spare hose and shirt folded there.

Hearing the clop and scrape of horses' feet out in the yard, she laced the pack up tight again, and carried it out to where John and William stood ready to make their farewell.

John embraced Madeleine, then was up in the saddle. William took his wife in his arms. 'I'll not be long,' he murmured, 'my dearest love.' And he pressed his lips in tenderness to her brow, holding her close to him before he mounted the palfrey standing patiently there at his side.

'What's your horse's name?' she had asked him, when first they met. She had laughed at the name – Nightmare – when he told her then. She understood, now she knew more about the history of the man who chose the name, how easily that might have sprung to mind.

As she opened the gate and held it for them to pass through, calling a farewell after them before she turned back to the chores of the afternoon, Madeleine reflected on the complicated weather of William's inner world. She did not understand him, she concluded as she usually did; but nevertheless, he was the only man for her, and always would be.

✠   ✠   ✠

'So, what is it? What's wrong?' John asked into the silence between them.

'Nay, I'm well,' William responded with carefully casual ease, sitting his horse gracefully as they ambled along the track that climbed up from the valley. 'I keep remarkably well. I've had no further problems with my chest this winter, which I wondered if I might – pneumonia leaves a permanent weakness, so I've heard. Brother Michael said I must always take care to keep warm and keep out of the draughts. But I've kept well.'

When his words ceased, for a while the creak of leather and the steady multiple tread of their horses' hooves on the turf were the only sounds. And the harsh cawing of a crow perched on the winter-bare branch of a small tree grown out of true by the insistence of the prevailing wind.

'Oh, come on, William! Don't lie to me!'

Again the silence, the steady beat of the horses' feet, the creak of the saddles.

'Abbot John Hazell, you have healer's eyes and you know me too well, both of which are unfair advantages.'

Tread. Creak. Tread. Creak. Tread. Creak.

'Are you going to tell me, then? Is all not well between you and Madeleine?'

William moved his head, hunted, exasperated, cornered.

'Madeleine is more willing to be patient with me than most would be,' he said eventually. 'Our situation is such as to find out all my inadequacies. I never imagined a man could spend such a disproportionate amount of time thinking about firewood and mud. Every new day brings me face to face with the need for skills I have never learned. I can eat my fair share of the bread of humiliation, and I'm certainly used to its flavour by this time, but it gives a man a bit of a bellyache nonetheless. That's all you've seen, nothing serious. It gets me down at times, is all.'

'I see. Well, where we're going now you will certainly find yourself both skilled and handy. No mistake about it, we sorely need your guidance and your help.'

'Aye, well that of itself is a gift to me. I'm grateful to be of service.'

'So… there is nothing else? Nothing amiss? Nothing troubling you? You seem out of sorts to me. Look, William, Madeleine's my sister. I grew up with her. I know her like myself. She is the truest, kindest soul – and she can also be devastatingly honest, witheringly scornful, over particular, very dismissive, and she will never let *anything* go. Are you trying to tell me you're finding that easy to live with?'

Tread. Creak. Tread. Tread. Creak. Tread. William felt his friend's perspicacious gaze on him; kind, teasing, gentle.

'Aye, she can be all of that.' He paused. 'Married life,' he admitted eventually, 'with Madeleine, is like a precarious walk along the top of a hurdle never made to bear a man's weight, while one person pelts you with cabbages and another intermittently takes you by surprise throwing a bucket of cold water in your face. Never dull. But it's easy enough to complain. What about me? You've lived with me too, and was that an easy ride?'

John laughed. 'It was not! Well, it's been a year and the two of you are still married, and it's me begging you to come back and help us, not you beseeching me to take you in. I've heard people say the first year of marriage is the hardest. Novitiate struggles, I guess. So, all's well? Truly?'

William hesitated. 'It hasn't been the best week in our marriage. We're all right, but... I... a number of things... not the least of which was...'

John waited, saying nothing, watching William's face tighten into a mask.

'I broke the bread bowl that Brother Thaddeus made.'

He said it steadily, with absolute control; but then his jaw clenched and his mouth hardened into a bloodless line, and he said no more, focusing hard on the palfrey's ears.

John smiled. 'And Madeleine was upset?'

William neither replied nor looked at him; he merely nodded in affirmation.

'Oh. Well, that's no matter. I'm glad you told me. Bowls are only made out of clay, and Brother Thaddeus has nothing to do but make pots from it. He can make you another. I'll ask him when we get home. It'll be the least we can do, putting yourself to all this trouble to come and help us.'

He spoke gently. William reined in his mount, and sat completely still, his hand raised to his eyes and pressed hard against them.

'Stop it, John,' he mumbled after a moment, John having paused alongside him, waiting. 'How do you do this? How do you always *get* to me? You un-man me completely – you and Madeleine both! There is no hiding place from either of you!'

His breath drew in sharp and ragged, but he made the necessary effort to gain mastery over himself, dropped his hand to the saddle pommel again and, with a squeeze of his knees and nudge from his feet, set his palfrey once more in motion.

He turned his head to look at John. 'Can we talk about something else? Anything that's not me. Tell me something to help me look at the present state of the community household. Have you any special work in hand?'

'No, we bumble along as usual. The money that came to us from Mother Cottingham put us back into a manageable position, and you had identified for us the supplies we were lacking, which Brother Ambrose was able to order in before he died, happily, using the extra money. Things are fairly quiet now, between Martinmas and Easter. Not many guests. Although – oh, yes, I should tell you about that – there is one small thing afoot. Lady Agnes d'Ebassier took it into her head that it would be lovely for her sisters – she has five sisters – each to have an identical copy of the Book of Hours we made for her, and she wants to present them to her sisters at the feast of the Blessed Virgin Mary in May. So we've needed to order in a quantity of gold and more pigments for ink, and some better vellum than we had. Father James is going to make some corners and clasps for us in chased silver. Everyone in the scriptorium, and a number of men who aren't, has been busy on that. Father Theodore graciously gave us every hour he could spare from the novitiate – he's the best of us at the illuminated capitals and illustrations by a long way. Anyone at a loose end has been sent along to the scriptorium to help with the task. Father Clement said Father Francis could do some of the pages of the office of None, because he says everybody falls asleep in None so they won't pay much attention to what they're reading – which I thought was more waspish than he needed to be. He won't let him paint the illuminations, but agreed he could fill in the capital. I'm surprised Francis wanted to do it at all, in fact, after Clement had finished detailing his caveats and provisos, but Father Francis is a gracious man. I sent Brother Thomas along, but he was back almost before I knew it, saying, "Father Clement asks me to pass on to you that I should know by now there's no 'h' in 'coelis' and don't bother to send me again." It's been an expensive project but should bring a good return. We haven't talked about Lady Agnes paying us for them, but there's no doubt in my mind Sir Geoffrey will make us a more than generous gift – he always does.

'That's the only major thing happening with us, except the bishop's Visitation in May – and in the same month Brother Damian's sister is to be married from the abbey, but that should be straightforward enough.'

'Brother Damian's sister? The voluptuous Hannah? Hannah with the goats?'

'Aye, Hannah. You remember her?'

'She's something of a gleaner, is Hannah. She was often in the checker begging and wheedling for any odds and ends we might have to give away, or for a vial of Brother Walafrid's drenches for her animals. If you'd sat as I did, at the table in the checker, with Hannah standing on the other side of it leaning over, you'd remember her too. You'd have been proud of me, John. I kept my eyes steadily on her face.'

John grinned. 'Mmm, yes, I guess she is quite memorable.'

'And she's to be wed? She has two or three children already, doesn't she?'

'Aye, indeed – two. It's not that she's free with her favours, but I think there's been some difficulty in winning the acceptance of her man's family. They're higher born than Brother Damian's people, and I gather they'd hoped for a better match than Hannah. Still, they must have been won over at last. I could have done with it being a different month from the bishop's Visitation, but there we are – I don't suppose it'll amount to much. Nothing else presses urgently – yet – but you know how life goes. You don't need me to explain. And then... well... you say *your* situation ferrets out your inadequacies – do you not imagine the same is true for me? In all honesty, I would not have conjectured the whole of Christendom and the lands of the Saracen combined yielded as much administration as we can come up with in our abbey, modest in size though we be. Oh, heaven, and... during the autumn...'

William listened with interest to his friend as their mounts walked easy along the track, picking a way past puddled ruts and occasional fallen branches or tumbled stones; but in this pause he detected distress, and his shrewd sideways glance saw something momentarily shaky and appalled about John's mouth, and a memory of trauma in his eyes.

'... We had need of pointing the tower at St Mary the Virgin – I don't know what it is with that building, they cannot seem to hold it all in one piece for five minutes together – and it seemed wise while we had money in hand to see it right. But... it was when they were putting the scaffold up... they wanted to work with ladders but I was afraid for them falling, and said they must build a scaffold. And while they were erecting it, a man slipped from a ladder perched all precarious there, no sandbag weighting the bottom, nobody holding it steady. Right from the top. Four children and one on the way at home, and he broke his back in the fall – he fell awkward against the gravestone there. By God's mercy he lived... at least I say that, but... what's his wife to do with a man bedridden for good and all, and more mouths than she knows how to feed on the wage he brought home already? I sat there when they told me of it, thinking how it must be for them in that tiny cottage... remembering my own mother with no more than two children, when the news came back that my father – he was a soldier – had fallen in battle. I remembered the fear and uncertainty of it, not knowing whatever we would do without him to provide for us. And I just felt sick for them, thinking of it. It was dreadful. I felt so responsible.'

He fell silent.

'Aye, well,' William's dry, quiet voice broke into the misery of that memory, 'there's no man alive, abbot or anyone else, that has been able to accident-proof idiocy. What have you done for them? Promised them charity forever, if I know you. Am I right? Aye, I thought so! Abbot John, you do need a tougher cellarer and a shrewder prior, if only to protect you against yourself! The world is full of dolts and fools, and no doubt you have your fair share employed by St Alcuin's. You can't patch all their bruises and scrapes when they take a tumble. Oh, I know – I know! You don't need to give me that look! I haven't forgotten whose kindness saved me from myself and all my own folly – and you threw me a wife into the bargain, which was one kindness further than I think you meant! I'm grateful, and sensible of the difference goodness can make. I only meant you cannot rescue all of us; it isn't practical.'

He glanced sidelong at John's face, and relaxed. He preferred the irritation and lively indignation with which he found himself now regarded, to the look of helpless dismay about John's mouth that had lodged in William's viscera like a physical pain.

'Berate me!' He shrugged. 'Tell me I have no heart. Call me an ingrate! I'm only saying. The world's a-crawl with boneheads, and even you cannot take pity on 'em all.'

As they rode up the crest of the hill to where the land levelled out into the ground that cradled the abbey before rising into the moorland that wrapped it round, John reflected on how hard to read he found this man. In William's words he heard indifference, heartlessness even. Then why, in some elusive corner of his soul, in a manner he could not readily put his finger on to identify, did he feel obscurely comforted? Even stoutly loved. He left it. 'We're home,' he said, adding casually: 'I didn't tell anyone you'd be coming.'

As Brother Martin drew back the heavy bolt and opened the great door to allow their passage in, William caught the startled look of surprise on his face once he had got past the beard and recognized who rode as companion to his abbot. *Oh, here we go.* William reflected that for no man he esteemed less than John Hazell would he submit to the mixture of reactions he was likely now to encounter. Suspicion, embarrassment, resentment, dislike, hostility, astonishment – what would meet him here? He steeled himself for whatever it would be this time, dismounted, and turned to face Brother Martin.

'Your abbot tells me my help is needed,' he said simply. 'God give you good day, and I'm glad to be under Benedict's roof once again. For a day or two only, you'll be glad to hear.'

Brother Martin recovered himself enough to muster an adequately civil greeting. John watched this in amusement. William felt himself shrivelling under the prospect of more of the same; but he turned a bravely impassive face to his friend. 'What will you have me do? The sun's setting, they'll be ringing the Vespers bell any time soon. Should I… um… look – it will be a kindness if you let me wait for you in your lodging. Don't make me run the gauntlet of Brother Dominic and whoever else is in the guesthouse. I can take only so much startled what's-he-doing-here.'

John stopped, his eyes gazing thoughtfully into William's, a scrutiny that effected an uncomfortable squirming in William's belly. 'I see,' said John; and William knew that was true and wished it were not. 'Yes; come to my house.'

As they arrived at the door opening from the abbey court into the abbot's lodging, it felt strange to William to have the abbot step back in courtesy to allow William to precede him as his guest into his house. William's instinct still made him want to stand back in respect for his abbot. But John was no longer his abbot. This was no longer his home. It occurred to him as he crossed the threshold that, however eagerly he might have taken the chance to be of service, this would be a visit that churned up any amount of buried emotion left unexamined under the pressure of having enough to cope with as he struggled to accommodate to ordinary domestic day-to-day existence. His apprehensions had no chance to develop into full-blown foreboding, though, because he and John were not alone in the abbot's house.

'Oh, well met! Right glad am I to see *thee*! But, faith, you look almost done in! 'Twasn't that hard a ride, was it? Has my abbot been battering you and burdening you with our troubles? Good to have you in this house once more! Are you well? Is married life suiting you?'

And William found himself clasped in a hearty bear-hug as Brother Thomas advanced beaming across the room to make him welcome. Grateful to the core, he gave himself to that unequivocal embrace, and Abbot John smiled contentedly as he picked up William's bag abandoned on the floor, and set it on the hearthstone where the fire his esquire had lit ready would steam out any vestiges of winter damp.

'Married life,' said William then in response to Tom's question, '– well, *my* marriage – is turning out to be, predominantly, one long apology.'

'Oh!' John smiled at him cheerfully. 'Not so very different from monastic life as you thought then, maybe?'

William shrugged. 'Nobody ever exclaimed, "Not like that, you great lummock!" in my years of religious profession, that I recall – and, Brother Thomas, I *saw* that grin!'

'*Mea culpa*,' murmured the abbot's esquire, but his expression was not entirely penitent.

At William's request, John gave him a lantern and the key to the checker, so William could look over the present state of the books in what remained of the afternoon. John invited him to join the community for Vespers, but that he declined, saying that he would need to make the most of the time he had and preferred not to leave Madeleine to fend for herself at home for longer than he had to in this season of darkness. He thought if he worked fast and could examine the accounts in the remnants of this day, then spend perhaps two days asking questions of the different obedientiaries, he could form a good grasp of what needed to be done, and communicate that to Abbot John. If he then gave two and a half days to an initial instruction of Brother Cormac – assuming all went well on moving him from the kitchens to the checker – he could be home by dusk in five days' time. His conscience smote him. That was a long time to leave a woman to manage alone and unprotected: but however focused his approach, he didn't see how he could any further shorten the time.

This early in the year when dusk crept in by mid-afternoon, and the sun set at four, the brothers kept more to the house than in the summer, and visitors were few. So he worked alone and uninterrupted, but did not delude himself that meant his presence went unremarked. He could stay clear of Vespers and Compline if he liked, but he might as well go to Mass in the morning, because by that time the whole community would know he was there.

He worked in the checker until supper time, bringing the rent records and the last trade ledger across to the abbot's house to peruse when they had eaten. He had covered too little ground as yet to give him anything to discuss. The warmth of Tom's and John's friendliness as they ate together – John invited Tom to sit down and share supper with them – touched his soul like balm. Despite his concerns about Madeleine and apprehension lest he be less than universally welcome, William relaxed. It was good to be back here again.

Tom left them after they had dined. John gave his big oak table to accommodate William's spread of accounts, fetching the scribe's table from its now very dark nook by the wall nearer to the fire and lantern light to prepare for his homily in the morning.

'What are you talking to them about?' asked William.

'The breath of peace,' John replied. 'How Jesus came to his disciples as they were gathered together – so flawed and vulnerable, so fearful – and said to them, "Peace be with you," and breathed into them his gift of the Spirit... courage... hope... life... I've been pondering on that – you know, thinking about the power of his words to the disciples: how they must have remembered that conversation, carried it with them. And the other thing he said, earlier on in the gospel: "... *pacem relinquo vobis pacem meam do vobis non quomodo mundus dat ego do vobis non turbetur cor vestrum neque formidet*"... um... peace I leave with you, my peace I give to you, don't be troubled of heart, don't be frightened."

Yes, I do know what it means, thought William, but even as the words went through his mind he recognized his testy response as the reflex of defensiveness; he wanted to find his way to that peace again so much that the longing felt like a pain.

'I thought how what he said must have comforted and strengthened them so,' John continued, musing aloud. 'It must have worked on the formation of the men they would become. And then that led me on to wonder about the power of our words – yours and mine – and about the influence of memory and the deep roots it has in a man; the awesome responsibility of leadership as an abbot... a novice master... a parent; how much it matters how we nurture and shelter the ones entrusted to our care... especially, though not only, the young ones – the novices, the postulants, the children here in our school. Especially them, because how we treat the child determines the man he will become. But not them only, because there is a sense in which we are all still children inside. That means that there are second chances, maybe, to grow something new; but it also means we do well to touch the soul of a man with tenderness, remembering that whatever else he is, he is somewhere also a child. Thinking that, if we use our breath for words of peace and kindness, maybe it will be the moving of the Holy Spirit in a life here and there – catching something of that breath of Jesus and his legacy of peace. But I don't think I want to cram all that into tomorrow's abbot's Chapter. I'm only rambling.'

William, watching him with the intensity of a hunting wildcat, said nothing. Slightly embarrassed, John smiled. He thought he would never get used to the improbable notion of himself holding forth on a daily basis for the edification of his community. The kind of thing that would have made him laugh if it hadn't been such a terrifying responsibility. Self-conscious, he picked up the stylus to note down chapter and verse, and William redirected his attention to the perusal of the records spread out before him.

As they worked in companionable silence William's presence, so unobtrusive and entirely soundless, emitting nothing to distract or disturb, reminded John of the days of his own deep grief in bereavement, when the only man he could bear to have near him for any length of time was William, for that very quality of quietness. John's memory trod gingerly into that difficult territory of his life – as much of it as he could remember, for he found great blank spaces there as well. But he recalled with gratitude William's immoveable, implacable defence against the anxious interference of Father Chad… *Father Chad…*

'Oh! Lord! William!' His friend looked up, one eyebrow lifted in enquiry.

'I wanted to pick your brains about finding a new prior. I took note of what you said, and you're absolutely right, and it's something I know I must face up to. But I've got the same problem as I had over the obedience of cellarer. I just don't know who to ask. I must say we do seem to be hard up for leadership material.'

William listened to him thoughtfully. 'Leadership?' he said. 'There are few natural leaders among men, and those there are can be a confounded nuisance in a community, if you don't manage to direct their gifts and graces along the right channels. Men grow into leadership. It's only a matter of confidence and familiarity with the job. Well – provided you pick the right man in the first place, of course. You have nobody in mind?'

'Er… no. That is – Germanus has been doing nothing in

particular. He's an intelligent man, and he should be priested, but... the prior... no; short answer is I don't know.'

'Oh. Well, if I were you I would ask Father Francis.'

Surprised and intrigued, John turned this proposition over in his mind. 'Francis... I would never have thought... why Francis?' he said.

'The mere fact that he's so thoroughly able but everyone overlooks him is a good start,' his friend replied. 'In a prior you need a man content with second place; someone personable, and capable of making a decision without panicking, but who doesn't mind being in the background – and you won't find that combination often. He's charming, he's unfailingly sweet-natured, he upsets nobody – all in addition to being a perceptive, intelligent man who can stand his own ground when the need arises. I've noticed he doesn't always flow with the current or speak with the popular voice. Besides, he's an excellent foil to Brother Cormac who is *not* charming or unfailingly sweet-natured and who manages to upset everybody. With Francis on your right and Cormac at your left you couldn't lose. Francis can disarm your enemies while Cormac watches your back. And while we're on this subject, I never thought to ask: Brother Conradus – he is professed now, is he not? If you take Cormac out of the kitchen, you won't have to be finding someone to plug the gap before he makes his solemn vows?'

'No, no. He'd made his simple vows already when you came here. He made his solemn profession during this last year. But he will need help, and he's too young in the life for it to be prudent to set a novice to work alongside him.'

'Brother Giles, maybe? He seems a steady man, and Brother Walafrid's not so overburdened with work he really needs an assistant.'

'Oh – good thought! Yes. Brother Giles would do admirably. You know, I'd run this place just fine if I always had you sitting on my shoulder telling me what to do.'

'You think so? Can I hold you to that next time you're raging at me for breaking every rule in the book in flagrant disregard for Benedictine tradition?'

John smiled. 'I think I have been too harsh in my handling of you at times, and not always perceptive enough. Our Father Matthew...' John picked his way carefully, mindful that he was the abbot of his community and did himself no credit by offering himself as their detractor, 'died some years ago now, but he was once the novice master here. Father Matthew had a very tender conscience. He... he could be quick to identify the faults of those under his authority. He was often correct in his observations, but he did not always get to the heart of the matter, which sometimes could make bad things worse.'

William listened to this careful assessment, amusement gleaming in his eyes. 'I see,' he said. 'No prophet, and no loss either?'

John grinned at him. 'Go back to your accounts! Father Francis... yes. The more I think of that, the better I like it. Thank you.'

As the Compline bell rang, John realized he had done nothing about finding William a bed in the guesthouse. 'Oh, don't you worry,' said William casually. 'I have my cloak and my pack for a pillow. I'll bed down here at your hearth – provided you promise not to tread on me on your way through to Matins.'

On the verge of protesting, it dawned on John that the oversight had not been shared. William, leery of curiosity and disapproval, had said nothing to recall the abbot's mind to his sleeping quarters. He noted the familiar flicker of reticence in William's eyes under the exposure of discernment and compassion. He nodded. 'If you'll take one of my blankets,' he said.

William's hand moved in concerned protest: 'Oh no, no – you'll be cold!'

'Then so will you. You have your cloak. I have mine. We shall have a blanket each. Brother, the floor is draughty. You take it or I'll hook Dominic out of silence to find you a bed in the guesthouse. Which is it to be?'

Brother… William stowed the treasure in his heart. 'All right,' he said. 'Thank you. I – if you don't mind, that is – I won't come to Compline. Let the grapevine do its work. I'll come to Mass in the morning. And… well…' He paused awkwardly. 'Look – I won't embarrass you. I might come to the altar for a blessing, but maybe not even that. I do understand that you can't offer me the host. I haven't forgotten.'

No, thought John, recognizing the pain of this exclusion: *I don't suppose you have.* He had not enquired what William did about the eucharist in his new home – mingled with all the others and let his identity be lost in the crowd, he supposed. But here, where he was known all too well as a brother who had forsaken his solemn vows, he could not ask to be included in the communion of Christ's fellowship. *Ow…* the severity of that hurt cut into John's soul like a sharpened knife. Lost for words, he just stood and looked at his friend.

'No!' William shook his head. 'Leave it be – I brought it on myself – it's all right. Go. You'll be late. I'll fetch a blanket from your bed like you said, and tuck down here by the fire when I'm done. Don't pity me, John – I'm not worth it. Look, get you gone.'

But John still stood there. 'There are two ways to communion with Christ,' he said. 'One is to receive the *Corpus Christi*, the other is to be it. No one can take that away from you.'

'The bell's stopped ringing. Go.' And William turned away.

In the morning when the community met for Chapter, the abbot made the brothers officially aware of William's presence. He explained why William had come, and that he would be among them for a few days to determine the state of matters awaiting their new cellarer, whose identity would be decided during those few days. Another visit no doubt would be required in the busier and more challenging times later on in the spring. He asked that William be made welcome as he did the rounds of the abbey, making inventories, asking questions, drawing all into readiness for the new obedientiary.

'I am more grateful to him than I can say,' said the abbot firmly, to quell any resentment before it had time to build. 'The hole we're in now is of my making, and he didn't have to come and help us out of it. Do your best to assist him.' *Be kind...* he wanted to add; but he hoped he didn't have to.

After Chapter he found William in the checker, bringing the bills and receipts accumulated since Brother Ambrose's death into date order ready to be dealt with later. William set the task aside to walk round the abbey with John, hearing the abbot's observations about changes made or still waiting to be done.

'I notice you have fires on every hearth,' William remarked. 'Nay, don't look so guilty! It's good for morale and does something towards keeping mildew out of the books, rot out of the wood, and stopping men falling sick. But I'm surprised there's a tree left standing in the north of England, the amount you must be burning here. What's your fuel bill been? You don't know? But... you must have signed off the payments, surely?'

Then, seeing John's embarrassment and sense of inadequacy, he added quickly: 'No, look, it's me – it's not you. I can't help memorizing costs and prices – most people don't. I'll look it up when I get back into the checker. May I take a lantern and go in again tonight? I'll use the daylight hours to find out what I need from the brothers. And as for trying to alleviate the cold as best you can, well, I did the same thing in your position. D'you think we were cold at St Dunstan's? I'm surprised we didn't burn the place down even with no one to help us, the great fires we had roaring away on a winter's day!

'There now, I won't take up any more of your time – you've shown me what I need to see. I'll just prowl about a bit and ask the right questions. Maybe wait until tomorrow to ask Brother Cormac? Just to be sure we have the right man for the job? Yes? Good. I'll see you later on.'

Chapter Four

'Concept,' said Brother Conradus, the generous contours of his amply proportioned figure whisking vigorously about the kitchen with remarkable agility through sheer force of irritation. 'A man comes in here between meal-times because he has missed his dinner, or has a guest, or just feels hungry. He helps himself to bread and butter and honey, maybe to a slice or two of cold pigeon, or a wedge of left-over stuffing, or a drink of ale or a hunk of cheese. And he is welcome to it. We are not stingy here. Then, when he has done, he takes the plate, the bowl, the knife, the spoon, the mug – whatever he has used – and he *washes it up and puts it away*! Is that hard to grasp, as an idea? I think not. Is it asking a lot of him? I hadn't thought so. Is it difficult to do? Nay, not so, apparently. Not difficult at all. *Impossible!*

'Same with dirty linen. Cloths for straining cheese, we rinse through thoroughly, of course; likewise if we have strained fruit or anything else, or cooked a pudding in them or whatever. Rags from washing and drying dishes and wiping down the table, we rinse out crumbs and anything stuck to them. Then the cloths go on the heap yonder by the door waiting for whoever goes by to take them to be laundered. And who do you think it is that takes them? Guess! Why – me or Brother Cormac, *every time*! I say this to Brother Cormac and he laughs at me; tells me I'm being precious, and possessive, and – he did say this, he actually did –

bossy! But I say, this is community; you *help*, you *notice*, you *lend a hand*.'

William listened to this outburst with interest and amusement. He had never seen Brother Conradus look so thoroughly flustered and cross.

'Is that what your mother used to say?' he asked casually.

Brother Conradus stopped. 'Why, yes,' he answered in surprise. 'How did you know?'

William shook his head. 'No idea. It was just a thought that came to me.'

Satisfied that all seemed in order in the kitchens – that no knives or spoons had been lost, every pot and kettle kept in good repair, the stores used methodically not randomly – William had thought it might be wise to probe a little for information about the kitcheners. He had wondered how confident Brother Conradus would feel without the sheltering authority of Brother Cormac, and wanted to be sure he had overlooked nothing, could glean no final stray fragments of insight, before the abbot committed himself to moving Cormac to the checker. So he sat now in the kitchen in the quietness of the afternoon, looking through their record of stores and bringing them up to date, while at the same time chatting amiably to Brother Conradus, encouraging him to talk about his role as a kitchener and about the brothers alongside whom he worked.

William recognized that he had a unique advantage in having been part of the community. Brother Conradus felt less guarded than he would have done with an ordinary guest to the abbey – who would not have been inside the claustral buildings and sitting in his kitchen anyway. William's presence here implied the trust of the abbot, special permission granted, and Brother Conradus relaxed in the knowledge of this trust.

He glanced at William sitting at the table on one of the battered kitchen stools, updating the record of how many cords of wood they had used, how much flour and oil and salt.

'Are you... are you happier now?' he asked shyly. 'Did you... I heard... I think you may have married somebody?'

William looked up from the ledger, smiling a reassurance at Conradus's diffidence and his careful reticence lest he be gossiping or intruding.

'I married Madeleine Hazell.'

'Oh!' Brother Conradus's face cleared in understanding. 'Oh, I see! *That* love!'

'I beg your pardon?'

'Well – I'm not sure I should be saying this, and I'm not meaning to boast or pretend to be especially spiritual – but I used to pray for you so hard when you were here with us and so wretchedly unhappy. I asked Our Lady of Sorrows to pray to our Lord with me, because I didn't know what was the matter. I had no idea how to pray for you, or what petition to offer. And you know how it is in the novitiate. None of us knew and nobody was about to tell us. Then, as I was praying one day, the notion came to me that I should beg of God that you might have the courage to keep the flower of your love alive through this winter, for it would have its time in the sun. I had absolutely no idea what that meant. But it's what I used to pray for you. Madeleine Hazell. That must have been what Our Lady meant.'

Surprised and touched, William took this in, watching Conradus assemble the honey and spices, the butter, the lard and the flour. 'Thank you so much,' said William. 'Thank you for praying for me.'

Silence fell between them then, and he dipped the quill in the ink, returning to copying neatly into the book from the notes he had scratched into the wax tablet.

'I'd be grateful of your prayers again,' he admitted after a few minutes, without lifting his eyes from the inventory. 'I am indeed happier than I was, and glad I made the decision I did; but I won't pretend it's been easy. There seems to be so many bones of contention between us. Nothing ill-meant, not full-on rows exactly – just touchiness and picking at each other. Sometimes… there are days when I feel I can't say a thing right.'

Brother Conradus listened with sympathy to this confession as the shortening and flour cascaded light from his fingers rubbing in the butter and lard for the pastry.

'Ah! Don't I know that one! Most certainly I will pray for you. Oh, my word, that brings back memories! This is where the silence of our Rule is such a blessing – *such* a blessing! When people set out to live together in the ordinary way, with no silence for them to take refuge in, there's a tendency to just let slip any thought that's passing through their heads. So, for instance, I might happen to pass a remark to my sister: "You know, that green cap really isn't your colour." And then I'd think nothing further about it – or if I did, maybe even feel I'd done her a kindness in setting her straight, never realizing that she felt really hurt and spent the whole of the day stewing about it until she was half ready to kill me by suppertime. Then I'd make some innocent request – "Pass the pepper", or some such, and she'd let fly at me in a manner that seemed altogether uncalled for.

'My mother told us we had to guard against carelessness in the way we spoke to one another, for she said that's all it was; but I think the Grand Silence works a treat – it gives us the space we need to think better of our indiscretions and contemplate the possible consequence of some of the things we've said, or could've said and didn't.'

William nodded thoughtfully as he considered this, the pen idle in his hand as he watched the deft movement of Conradus's fingers reducing the whole big bowlful of wheatflour and dollops of fat to fine sprinkling particles like powdery breadcrumbs.

'"Let fly" is exactly right. I love Madeleine so much, but I seem to be forever hurting her without meaning to. And… I take a fair few bruises of my own from every fray. That is – I mean, we don't hit each other, it's not like that with us. Just words that sting and tear. Without ever intending to at all. It... hurts.'

Brother Conradus smiled at him, a flash of perceptive merriment full of kindness and understanding.

'Oh, I know that so well! Painful, isn't it! But my mother says it's nothing more than self-pity, which will evaporate by itself if we ignore it.'

William reflected that Brother Conradus's mother seemed to have been a source of wisdom on every possible manifestation of human dilemma, and was on the verge of saying so when he suddenly caught himself. He realized how acid the remark would sound, and recognized that this sourness that came so readily had probably poisoned more conversations than he cared to admit in the course of his new vocation as a husband.

'Self-pity,' he said thoughtfully, instead. 'She's probably right.'

In silence he watched Conradus judge with practised ease the precise amount of cold water to add to the dry ingredients, draw the mixture together with the minimum of mess, then turn it out to knead quickly and lightly with his fingertips on the floured board.

Then recollecting the purpose of his visit and banishing the inclination to brood on his domestic disharmony, William set himself to casually drawing Brother Conradus into a consideration of the running of the kitchen, commenting admiringly on Brother Cormac's willingness to accommodate Brother Conradus's superior culinary talents, and the affability with which they worked alongside each other. He touched on this and that aspect of the work the kitcheners shared together, asking questions, making observations, listening astutely to every contribution Brother Conradus made to the conversation without ever allowing him to feel this was more than rambling inconsequential chitchat to pass the time.

The young man was cautious and kind in what he said, adroitly sidestepping any assessment of Brother Cormac's performance in the creation of comestibles, until William with apparently artless and ingenuous interest touched upon the subject of making sauces – a skill dear to Conradus's heart and the cause of a great deal of firmly repressed vexation. Cormac's sauces, lumpy and erratically seasoned, were in his estimation not far off inedible.

'Oh, yes,' said Brother Conradus, 'gray-vy. It's all in the name!'

He stopped dead then, a slow flush of embarrassment further reddening his already rosy cheeks under the kindling amusement of William's gaze. Conradus was a loyal soul as well as kind. He could hardly believe that he had let his tongue run away with him as he indulged in this idle prattle and allowed himself the indulgence of so sarcastic and critical a remark. He had thought all kinds of caustic things about Brother Cormac's culinary efforts, but never before had he permitted himself to give voice to such uncharitable opinions. Since William was no longer a brother of his house, he had not even recourse to the kneeling confession of his sin of scorn and contempt, and the forgiveness that would set the matter right.

'I can't believe I just said that,' he muttered, shaking his head as he wiped the mouth of the jar of honey, stoppered it, and took it back to the pantry.

William, intrigued and amused, said nothing, watching him quietly.

'This is the whole problem with sitting about gossiping! Father Theodore could have told me that…'

Or your mother, William thought.

'Or my mother!' exclaimed Brother Conradus.

'It's my fault,' said William contritely. 'I'll leave you in peace. And I don't think you're being uncharitable. I've eaten Cormac's gravy. Honesty's not such a bad thing.'

But Conradus shook his head, disgusted at himself, his lips sealed against further indiscretion. William saw it really was time he went, murmured his farewell, tidied away the record books and writing implements with no further comment and slipped unobtrusively out of the kitchen. He had what he wanted; he felt confident he could report to Abbot John that not only would moving Cormac out of the kitchen do no harm, it would actually avert the development of a problem as Conradus grew in confidence here in his natural domain. Feeding the community was, William could see, Conradus's great masterpiece of love, just as sweetening the lives of the aged and sick was Brother Michael's. It seemed, he thought, not insignificant that during the brief tranquillity of the afternoon Brother Conradus could be found attending to this and that small task left outstanding in the kitchen as often as Brother Cormac could be found somewhere else.

Satisfied with what he had seen, William moved on to the infirmary, and then to the sacristy, the pottery, the scriptorium and the robing room, asking questions, checking supplies, and gathering into one orderly complex pattern held together in his mind the present state of the affairs of St Alcuin's, in readiness for introducing the as yet unsuspecting future cellarer to the intricate matrix of the abbey's web of enterprises.

He had yet to go through the same process of investigation with the school, and make a systematic check of the bulky records covering St Alcuin's substantial responsibilities and transactions as a landlord. He would give over the day to those matters from first light tomorrow; and by the following day he would be ready to take Cormac through the first steps of the overview he must begin to absorb.

After Vespers, William joined the abbot for supper, apprising him of the ground he had covered during the day and the matters still awaiting his attention. Pleased and slightly astonished at the areas of the abbey's life William had checked in one day, John nonetheless refrained from asking any searching questions in the presence of Brother Thomas waiting on their table, lest

William should have uncovered any matters best confided to the abbot alone. But even the initial outline gave him cause for encouragement and reassurance that their current predicament had found its solution. As Brother Tom came to William's side to replenish his cup of wine – which William declined; he wanted a clear and alert state of mind to take the abbot through all the information he had gathered – John saw the warmth and approval in Tom's eyes. The observations Tom had made about William when first he had arrived on their doorstep begging refuge almost two years ago had been so violently hostile John thought it unlikely he would ever forget them. Watching Tom's face now, a sense of gratitude and satisfaction welled up in him as he marvelled at the distance travelled and the change achieved. It was, he thought, in a human way, a kind of miracle.

When they had concluded their evening meal, Tom withdrew from the abbot's lodging, taking the platters and bowls and eating irons back to the kitchen where he left them to soak for Brother Conradus to deal with in the morning. Abbot John invited his guest to the fireside, where uninterrupted he could hear the detail of William's assessment of the present state of things, and the advice that arose from his careful examination. As he concentrated on William's observations, John felt that at last, seeing the temporal concerns of the abbey's life through the lens of William's cool judgment and practical mind, he was himself beginning to obtain a more confident grasp on the matters that not only the cellarer but also the abbot should hold clearly in sight.

He listened, he questioned, he sought clarification here and there; and what had appeared difficult and daunting because it seemed so mysterious and vague, at last began to take shape for him. He felt immensely grateful to William. Turning it over in his mind in silence as he gazed into the low red flames curling sinuously from the ashy logs, he entertained a cautious hope that he might one day feel he had the measure of this aspect of the work entrusted to him.

'John, can I... can I ask you about something else for a minute? About me – us – me and Madeleine, I mean. I think I need your help.'

William ventured a glance at John to size up how the abbot might receive this, and saw that he had his friend's immediate and complete compassionate attention. Somewhere in the pit of his stomach he felt a sudden lurch as he saw the kindness with which he was beheld. It brought him unexpectedly to the edge of tears. He realized that this above all else was what he wanted. Kindness. Understanding. Sanctuary. Battle-weary, his soul hungered for peace to a degree that had become quite desperate.

'Go on,' said John. He waited, seeing that something had unsteadied William, who looked away into the glow of the fire, and did not immediately reply.

'In some ways,' William managed eventually, back in command of himself, 'we do well. As lovers, what is between us is beautiful – and I thank God for that, because it allows us to heal no end of rifts and squabbles. I love her – as much as ever I did and more, I love her. She is the moon and the stars to me. I believe she loves me too, and trusts me. It isn't that. But somehow we can't get to a place of harmony. We are always warring. Nothing goes very far before we hit a rock and everything goes flying. I never was so often in trouble since I was a child. And... Madeleine... well... I have no right to complain about this, but at any time of night or day she will make such dizzyingly frank observations about my shortcomings – just casually in conversation – as to knock me completely off balance. "You have the scariest eyes of any human being alive. I should think anyone you looked at would want to run away." That kind of thing.'

Miserable at the thought of it, he glanced at John. His gaze was arrested. John was laughing. He couldn't help it.

'What?'

'Oh, I'm so sorry, William! She's quite right!' He tried for a straight face and failed.

William shrugged. 'I guess it's funny if you're anyone but me. Brother Conradus said that's just how it *is* in families – without our way of silence containing the house, people say whatever passes through their heads, and you simply have to resign yourself to not taking it personally. He says his mother would say my problem is self-pity.'

That sobered John up. '*What?* You have been talking to *Brother Conradus* about your marital strife? William, what are you *doing?*'

William shook his head. 'No, I – well, I didn't mean to. He asked… oh, I don't know…' His voice faltered into silence.

John slapped his hand down on his thigh in vexed frustration. 'You can't *do* this! This is *exactly* what you did before! You *cannot* come here and rearrange our ways to suit your own purposes! William, that's the whole point of a community. What keeps it strong, what makes it a place of peace, is that we consent to abide by the ways of our tradition – they are the fortress of our souls. I cannot have you discussing your relationship with a woman with one of our young brothers – with any of the brothers! It will unsettle them. It will make them restless and set off hungers that were manageable and quiet. Oh, *Sancta Maria*! You will not learn, will you? I should never have let you back in here! I should have known better than to trust you!'

William would not meet John's furious glare, but he felt it as acutely as if he had seen it. Wretched, he sat gazing into the fire, wondering how it could be that whatever he did and wherever he went, he made everybody angry within the shortest possible space of time.

'I'm sorry,' he said. He buried his face in his hands and sat, motionless.

After a minute, John leaned toward him. 'Hey –' he said, firmly still but more gently, 'come on out. Look, it's no good. I simply cannot have you do this, and well you know it. Come on, now,' he insisted. He reached a hand across to William's knee, squeezed it kindly, patted it, then sat back in his chair, shaking his head in exasperation, but his ire cooling nonetheless.

'William. Come out from there. Talk to me.'

William lowered his hands and faced his friend, who saw the despair in his eyes, around his mouth. 'Don't send me away,' William whispered. 'Please don't send me away.' He struggled for a more normal tone of voice. 'John, at home there is nothing I can do well. Most of the time I feel incompetent and stupid. I forget things, I carry out tasks badly, I'm clumsy, I'm inept – and I *hate* it. I'm a lousy husband. But I can help you with this. It's something I can do well – and if I don't, I tell you, you'll be in no end of a muddle in a shorter time than you realize. Don't send me away, John. Please. I – please – I… I'm begging you… It… it's so peaceful here. I'll be gone anyway in a day or so. Just don't send me away.'

'Peaceful?' The abbot's gaze challenged his. 'Well, it is until you arrive.'

And then John saw the extent to which that hurt, and he felt sorry for having said it, and even in feeling sorry he recognized another manifestation of the inevitable turbulence of trying to interact with William. The abbot sighed. 'Sometimes I rue the day I ever laid eyes on you,' he said. 'You find your way to trouble with the effortless ease of a lifetime's practice. Yes, you can stay. There is no doubt in my mind I shall be cursing myself for having said so, but yes. You can stay but, so help me God, if you hurt the vocation of one of the sons of this house, I don't know what I'll do, but you'll regret it! William, hear this: you are not – repeat, *not* – to discuss your home life and your marriage with the brothers. Do you promise me?'

'Yes. For sure. And I'm sorry, I... Conradus always caught me off guard. He's so comfortable to be with, and so kind. Why can't I be like that?'

'I don't know. Scary-eye malady, I guess. So, anyway, you were saying – you and Madeleine have been fighting? That's not amazing. She fights with everyone, so do you. I did warn you, but you wouldn't listen – you were in love. She's not an easy woman.'

He saw a flash of annoyance in William's eye that he thought was an improvement on the misery it replaced.

'I'm sorry,' John said penitently, 'I invited you to tell me about the struggles you've been having and all I'm doing is scolding you and saying "What did you expect? I told you so." That's not good medicine, is it? All right; let's start again. Do you argue over anything in particular, or is it just the arguing itself?'

'I think...' William hesitated. 'I think, at least in part – for me – what does my head in is the memories.'

John frowned. 'Memories? Of what?'

'Oh, John, I am plagued by memories, scourged by memories – I am *infested* by memories. They invade my dreams, they climb all over me, they...' His voice tailed away and he shook his head, helpless, defeated. 'It's so paralysing. It...'

John waited, but nothing more was forthcoming.

'Would you like to tell me about some of these memories?' he asked gently. William turned his face towards him momentarily and John, seeing the bleak, lurid light in his eyes and the hard set of his features, thought they were both looking at hell.

'It's nothing I've not mentioned to you – just individual occasions from when I was a lad. Times when I was so frightened – I mean scared enough to soil myself – or times when violence escalated and the pain went beyond enduring... and the mockery and laughter, and... it shrivels me, puckers and burns the surface of my soul, burrows into me until I... John, I am not whole, I have no goodness in me... I have no sound judgment – I will always be rejected, because right at my soul's deep core is this writhing nest of adders. I look into me when I start awake from bad dreams some nights, and it's like a sheep with the blowfly – you lift back a flap of what you thought was simple fleece and there's a great craterous wound heaving with maggots devouring the poor beast alive.'

He sat for a while in silence, then he said: 'I cannot begin to tell you how draining it is – how much energy it takes to try and keep staving it all off, holding it at bay, limiting as far as I can the havoc and ruin it makes in my every interaction.'

'Then,' said John again, softly, 'would you like to tell me of some of these memories that scourge your soul and wear you down until you are exhausted? Shall we see if it may bring some relief to speak them out? I am your friend, but I am an abbot too, and Christ's priest. In telling me, you can allow what tortures the inside of you to seep out into the wounded side of Jesus.'

'*Jesus?* The last thing I want to do is sully *Jesus* with the defilement that poisons and taunts and drains the life out of me!'

'No – and you will not. Where his wounds touch your wounds you will be made clean again. I will not push you to it, but I think it may help to tell me of these memories if you can bear to.'

For a long while no more words passed between them; and then, haltingly and full of shame, William named and described the things that had been done to him, and the hurt, the humiliation, the despair. John said nothing at all, he reacted in no way whatsoever; he just listened with his whole attention, and William felt himself wrapped, even as the miserable, sordid stories bled out of him, in an immensity of cleansing, sheltering, ministering, healing love. He did not weep, though there were moments when John almost did as he heard the bitterness and palpable suffering that had lacerated and warped the child who had grown into the man, twisting him out of shape until he had no concept of what it was to live simply and comfortably with another human being.

'Even now,' William added, when the dismal, lightless, gruelling tale of his childhood was done, 'I keep forgetting how to love. I don't really know. I can only put in place what I have learned here, and keep on making the deliberate choice to let Christ open me up, even if it hurts sometimes.'

'I hardly know what to say to you,' John said into the silence littered with so much ugliness and cruelty and pain. 'How did you survive?'

'I joined the order of Augustinians,' William replied simply; 'because I could see some kind of refuge there. And whether it was God's mercy or sheer accident that I made it to the age when I could do that, I cannot judge. From that point on, survival has been easy – well, most of the time. But I do sometimes wonder if survival is good enough. You know – if it is really worthwhile.'

The infirmarian in John did not like the sound of this. As words ceased, and the men sat together looking into the dying fire, John turned over in his mind the difficulty William presented him. He saw, as the abbot of a monastery, very clearly, that this man was, and probably always would be, a liability. His fractured inner world made a perfect fingerprint of chaos on all his relationships. Association with him set up a bridge between the community and the anarchic discord of William's soul. John wondered what to do, and wondering turned instinctively to urgent, unspoken prayer. In the silence that lengthened between them, the words of the beautiful Gospel drifted into his mind: *Quis ex vobis homo qui habet centum oves et si perdiderit unam ex illis nonne dimittit nonaginta novem in deserto et vadit ad illam quae perierat donec inveniat illam...* What man among you, if he have a hundred sheep and one goes missing, will not leave the ninety and nine alone on the hillside, and go in search of the one? As an abbot, as an infirmarian, as anyone who even halfway pretended to follow Christ, he did not see that he had any kind of alternative. The broken whisper echoed again in his mind: *Please don't send me away.* But before he made the suggestion forming in his thoughts, he sought the heart of Christ, because he could see he was about to break all the rules again, and that with William as a travelling companion every way would lead inexorably to that same crossroads. He looked at his friend, and saw what the silence was doing to him. He saw defeat in the hard, tired lines of his face, the hopelessness of no solution that ever offered anything better than expediency.

'William,' he said, 'please remember how much you are loved. Madeleine loves you – and her interminable scolding is all part and parcel of her love, so you'll just have to live with that. I love you, and I am the abbot of this monastery, so you have to accept that in loving you I still must guard the boundaries. And others love you too; Tom – do you not remember his greeting yesterday? Michael. Theodore. Conradus. Possibly not Father Chad.' (William's face cracked into a grin as John said this last.) 'Love is better than survival and, though it has been freely given, you have earned it too. Now… Christ also loves you – you know that – and the love of Christ is touched and found in the eucharist. When we take into our bodies the bread and wine of the eucharist, we invite the presence of his light and life right into our very guts. No evil can co-exist with the presence of the living Christ. *Christus victor est.* Where he comes, he brings light and peace. You go to Mass, where you are living now – yes?'

William nodded. 'Aye. I do. And I would welcome the power of Christ into the gut of me, to put to death all that is evil in me – even if it killed me while he was doing it.'

'My friend, what I am about to suggest is that I go to the chapel for the reserve sacrament, and give you eucharist, and anoint you for healing and exorcism and blessing. Would you like me to do that?'

John registered the curious and unsettling sensation in his own belly that came from being held in William's gaze once his attention was caught. Like the gaze of a fox or a cat slowly advancing on an unsuspecting prey, completely focused. Single and silent and entirely inescapable. Not a comfortable experience.

'Exorcism and blessing?' William said eventually. 'You think...?'

'*No*,' said John decisively. 'I don't think anything – except that some truly devilish things have been done to you, and the echo of them has lodged in your heart and soul and, from what you say, drives you half crazy at times. I know of no power on earth that can lift such horrors out of you again, but I am trusting that the power of heaven may be equal to the job. That's all.'

William still watched him, and John felt him stalling, examining the idea. The sense of hesitation John picked up allowed him to feel less stalked, and allowed him to meet William's gaze with more equanimity. It was William who looked away, muttering, 'I thought you told me not to come to you for the eucharist. Because I broke my vows.'

'Aye, I did. But what can I do? Here you are, plagued and tormented by the demons of the past – eaten alive like a sheep with the blowfly. What's a shepherd to do when such a sheep comes to him in distress? Turn his back? Anyway, you were not excommunicated, though heaven knows you should have been. I would not refuse you the eucharist. Not here, in privacy. Well? What do you say?'

William, still with his head turned aside, nodded mutely. 'Thank you; yes,' he said, low and indistinct. And with no further ado Abbot John rose and went to fetch the reserve sacrament from the holy place at the back of the Lady Chapel altar.

'This,' he said, as he brought one of the stools to the fireside to serve as a table and laid out the fair linen cloth, the silver cross and the bread and wine, 'is the hope of humanity. This will heal you. This will make you clean. If you eat and drink this bread, this wine, discerning the body of Christ, it will be life to you.

Remember what Augustine taught his catechumens? When they received the bread from the priest into their hands, and heard the words "the body of Christ", they were to let their "Amen" be for "I am". The holiness that is Christ's is catching. When it touches you, it spreads within you. It will purge all rottenness and decay. It will touch the sore places of your spirit. It will turn you again to life. Is this what you want? Is this what you ask of Christ? William?'

Straightening up from arranging the holy vessels on the stool and turning back questioningly to his friend, the intensity with which he found himself beheld almost frightened John. *Holy Moses!* he thought. *No wonder everyone at St Dunstan's was terrified of him!*

'Oh, God, it's what I want more than anything.' The painful craving of the hoarse whisper felt no more reassuring than the pale feral glare of William's eyes.

John nodded, kissed and donned the purple stole, then stepped quickly across the room to fetch his breviary from the shelves behind the table. He came back to William, balancing the big book on his arm, turning the leaves of it to find the psalm he wanted.

'Will you repeat this after me, my brother, my friend?' Glancing up from the book John saw William's eyes flicker as he registered the word 'brother'.

'*Auditui meo dabis gaudium et lætitiam: et exsultabunt ossa humiliate,*' he read, and William obediently repeated the words. John traced his finger down the page, missing out a few verses to find the words he wanted: '*Ne projicias me a facie tua: et spiritum sanctum tuum ne auferas a me. Redde mihi lætitiam salutaris tui: et spiritu principali confirma me.*'

It was not hard for William to echo them back to him; every monk in Christendom knew those words from Psalm 51: *Make me to hear joy and gladness; that the bones which thou hast broken may rejoice… Cast me not away from thy presence; and take not thy holy spirit from me. Restore unto me the joy of thy salvation; and uphold me with thy free spirit.*

As William repeated the seventeenth verse, '*Sacrificium Deo spiritus contribulatus: cor contritum et humiliatum, Deus, non despicies,*' John paused and looked up from the book at him. 'Say it in your own mother tongue, William. Say it.'

'*The sacrifice of God is a troubled spirit. A broken and contrite heart, oh God, wilt Thou not despise.*' William whispered the words, his eyes full of brimming tears now, hardly able to speak. He bent his head.

'Do you believe that? Do you believe that word to us – to you?'

William hesitated. 'I hope it is true. Oh God, I do hope it is true.'

'Then shall we lift away some of the tarnish and accretions that time and life have gradually laid over the lamp of Christ in your soul? Shall we restore what you began with him?'

William raised his head, and it twisted John's heart with a sudden violence to encounter in his eyes the stubborn, brave child that had never grown up, never gone away, but inexplicably never quite given up either.

'After me, then: Beloved Jesus,' said John; and obediently, William whispered the words: 'My brother, my master, my friend… I have nothing to give thee but my troubled spirit… I love thee… I belong to thee… I put my trust in thee… Receive the sacrifice of this broken heart.'

It took some while for William to say those words in any form, but the tears that flowed then were not bitter or painful; they were the gift of Christ. As he opened his mouth to receive the broken host of the eucharist, his tears trickled in and mixed salty with the bread; his tears mixed with the wine and water of Christ's sacrifice.

'*Corpus Christi...*' said Abbot John, and William whispered, almost inaudibly, Augustine's 'I am'.

And then, taking the golden, fragrant oil, the abbot anointed him.

'*Reppele, Domini, virtutem diaboli, fallacesque ejus insidias amove: procul impius tentator aufugiat: sit nominis tui signo...*' His thumb dipped in the fragrant consecrated oil traced the sign of the cross on William's brow. '*... famulus tuus munitus et in animo tutus et corpore . Tu pectoris...*' William lowered his clasped hands to permit John to trace the cross of Christ on his breast. '*... hujus interna custodias. Tu viscera...*' Again John marked William's breast with the sign of Christ's love. '*... regas. Tu...*' His heart, the seat of his emotions, and now the courage of his intent: '*cor confirmes. In anima adversatricis potestatis tentamenta evanescent...*' And thus by the power of Christ conferred upon him John banished from his brother in Christ's family the taunting and tempting of the adversary; and he wondered if this should not have been done long ago.

'Will it always be like this?' William mumbled, when he could say anything, when all the prayers were done, the holy things stowed safely away, and they sat together by the falling embers of the fire once more. 'Clawing my way up out of the mess only to slip back in again and be mired in it until someone comes and helps me out?'

'I think it might,' said John gently, 'for you have been badly hurt at a time when who you are was growing and forming. But that's probably all right. So long as you know to come for help, and not ask too much of yourself. I think also, you should tell Madeleine, if you haven't already, of these terrors of memory when they assail you.'

William nodded. 'Yes. Maybe. She knows some. She asks about it when I have nightmares. But it's all so vile I hadn't wanted to...'

'I understand. But man and wife are one flesh, and it makes a space between you that creates bewilderment if unnamed ghosts and horrors locked in silence share your common life. I think if you have chosen to marry her, give yourself to her, then it has to be your whole self really. When you can. Not if it's just too much.'

The Compline bell began tolling then, and reflexively the two men moved in response to its call.

'Brother, what's been said here tonight – it is between you and me only; it is *not* for discussion with the brothers, any more than your marriage is. You are clear on that?'

Again William nodded, soberly. He understood indeed, fully aware of the extent to which John had crawled out on a very shaky limb for him, disregarding his ecclesiastical obligations to reject his renegade brother, in offering him the sacrament of Christ's welcoming love, the healing ordinance of his salvation. 'I understand very well,' he said. 'You can trust me, I promise. And I'm more grateful than I can say, for… well, everything really. Especially for a second chance. And for calling me "brother", which is gold and diamonds to me.'

William walked with Abbot John along the cloister to the chapel, holding precious the opportunity to sit with the brothers in choir. For the Mass, he had sat on the parish side of the altar, seeking only a blessing and not to receive the host when the time of communion came; and at Vespers he had sat among the more devout of the villagers – old women mostly – who observed the Hours as well as coming to hear Mass. But in the late, dark office of Compline, John had invited him to sit with the brothers; and the offer had been received like the crown jewels.

'Are you all right?' asked the abbot in an undertone, pausing as they reached the door of the church, while cloaked and cowled brothers padded past them to take their places in choir.

William's eyes gleamed in the reflected light of the cloister lanterns as he lifted his face, peaceful in spite of its haggard weariness, to his friend. 'I feel clean again. I feel whole again,' he replied.

✠   ✠   ✠

'Brother Thomas, there's no need to be on our dignity with these two – don't stay to wait on us, take your supper in the frater with your brothers.'

John spoke with his usual easy friendliness, but his esquire had reached the point by this time where he understood his abbot well. As he bowed in obedience and withdrew, Brother Tom wondered, walking along the cloister to the frater, why Father John wanted private audience with Cormac and William. There could not be many things he would prefer did not reach the ears of his esquire.

Brother Conradus usually took responsibility for the victuals that went to the abbot's table now. Brother Cormac's soul acknowledged in admiration that there was a reason for this, as he surveyed the array of very good cheeses, crisp savoury pastries, salad made out of stored apples and dried fruit and grated roots in the absence of greenstuff at this time of year, soused in dressing that Cormac knew would taste delectable. And, as always, perfectly salted butter and soft, well-risen bread. The realization came to him that, just as when William had been a brother with them he had been the cellarer in reality and Brother Ambrose held the obedience only in name, so it had come about that Brother Conradus was the kitchener in this house; he, Cormac, was tolerated there in kindness, not out of necessity. An uncomfortable thought, but he was grateful that they let him stay on in the kitchen; it was where he wanted to be.

Brother Cormac rose to his feet to pour his abbot and their guest their mugs of ale. He wondered why John had asked Brother Tom not to stay, but assumed that in such familiar company his own service at table would do just as well. So he tore the bread for them and cut into the cheeses, that partaking might be easier. John nodded his thanks, and Cormac resumed his seat.

'Do you have land, where you are?' he asked William. 'We had heard it's not too far from here.'

William nodded. 'Ten miles south-west. We have five acres. Good land. A stream runs through and we've a well, God be thanked. We have an orchard and some woodland that runs on into common woodland – good for our pig.'

'You keep a pig?'

William nodded and finished chewing the bread and cheese in his mouth. 'By heaven, this cheese is good, Brother Cormac! Yes, we do. We have hens too, not many – we also have a fox, but not by intention. We've started with just what we could manage, but we shall increase our little flock of hens by half a dozen as soon as we can, and I hope we'll be able to take on another goat this year.'

'Is it good land for growing?' John asked. 'Did your vegetables do well in the summer?'

As they consumed the tasty spread Brother Conradus had made them, William told them about the homesteading year that had passed, the crops they had grown, the fruit yield, and the plans they cherished for the year to come. An important factor in this was their sow, Lily, due to farrow sometime in March, whose offspring would give them a sucking pig to ease the lean gap of early spring, and hopefully provide income as well as food for their table – and maybe grow on a second sow to keep, to double the benefit next year.

'You plan to eat a sucking pig?' asked Brother Cormac. At these words a sense of foreboding stirred somewhere in the depths of John's soul.

'Aye, we do. Why?'

'It seems so sad.' Brother Cormac stopped eating, toyed with the torn bread still before him, glancing up momentarily at

William, then down at his plate again. 'Just a baby thing barely taken from its mother, never known the joy of life to run in the woods and rootle in the earth, scratch its back on a tree and feel the cool mud of a wallow when the sun is hot. Without even a chance at life. It seems so terribly sad.'

William shrugged. 'We'd eat the runkling. It would probably never make it through anyway, left to itself. 'Tis but following the course of nature, isn't it?'

'Aye, I suppose.' Cormac nodded, his face stilled with the sorrow of the prospect. 'What will happen to them? Not the one you keep for more pigs or the ones you sell, but the ones you keep to eat. Will you slaughter them yourself?'

William grimaced thoughtfully. 'I hadn't looked that far ahead. Possibly. Probably. I don't know.'

'Well, you should think about it,' said Cormac, and John heard a familiar note of peculiar intensity enter his voice, 'because it isn't that easy to kill a pig. Have you ever seen a pig killed?'

William had grown up in a town, and he had a queasiness about bloodshed. Unlike the other boys of his age, he had never joined the fascinated gathering to watch the awful sticking of a pig.

'Nay,' he said, 'I have not.'

'Killing a sheep or a goat is not so bad,' Brother Cormac persisted. 'You can gentle them, if they will come to you with no fear. You speak soft to them, and hold them, and they like it, they trust you. You have a sharp blade by, and a pail to catch the blood, and when you have lulled the beast all peaceful in your arms, you slit its throat right across. The throes are horrible, feet kicking in the dust; but it's a gentle death, and swift. But a pig is different.'

'Brother Cormac...' John murmured, noting that William's hand was trembling as he lifted his napkin and placed it on the table: but Cormac completely ignored the warning.

'It's not just the sticking, it's holding the pig. Pigs are strong and fast and nippy, besides which the strength in a pig's jaw can crunch your arm no trouble, and its teeth can tear your flesh to shreds. So when the man comes to stick the pig, once he's got it captive he has an iron to hold it. 'Tis a vile thing, a grisly spiked contraption to grip it by the snout – for their snouts are so sensitive, pigs. It screams and screams. And then the pigsticker with his knives and things, once he has a hold on it so painful it cannot get away, he plunges in the knife, and you will have to hold a bucket with oatmeal and cooked barley in right close, for the blood comes spurting out everywhere. It's a messy, bloody, cruel, screaming business, the death of a pig – and I envy you not one bit.'

Complete silence followed these words. William swallowed twice, convulsively. Even by candlelight his pallor was most evident. Abruptly he pushed back his chair, grabbed his napkin and made for the door to the abbey court, fumbling at the latch until he managed to get out, one hand pressing the napkin tight against his mouth.

'That was not helpful, brother,' chided Cormac's abbot quietly, as he rose to his feet to follow his guest into the night. Cormac said nothing, his expression settling into an unshakeable obstinacy with which John was all too well acquainted.

John took the lantern and found William not far outside, leaning against the wall, his forehead pressed gratefully against the cold stone, taking gulps of the night air. 'Be careful where you tread, I've just thrown up my supper,' he said, and groaned. 'I'll leave it lie, if you don't mind, and swill it down in the morning,' he added. 'Don't you worry, I'll come back inside in a moment. I'm all right, I just can't bear… Give me a minute. I'll be with you. I'm all right. Look – you're letting the cold in.'

Respecting his evident wish to be left in peace, John stepped back inside. 'Take this lantern,' he said to Brother Cormac, who stood when his abbot returned, 'and fetch a mug of cold water from the well. Direct from the well. Not something that's stood about in the kitchen gathering grease and dust.'

Perceiving himself to be in considerable disgrace, Cormac took the lantern and did his abbot's bidding swiftly. As he went he asked himself: was it wrong to have spoken so? Was it wrong to make a man think twice before he inflicted fear and agony on a beast and shed its blood? He could never understand why this always made people so angry – not with those who perpetrated the cruelty, but with him for making them think about it.

When he brought the water, he found William seated at the table once more. He offered him the mug, which William received thankfully, and took outside, that he might swill out his mouth and spit away the sour remnants of vomit.

'In the morning, first thing after Lauds before anyone has chance to step in the remains of Brother Conradus's fine repast outside on the pavement, you will kindly bring a pail of water and wash the stones clean,' said the abbot to Brother Cormac, who nodded in submission: 'Aye, Father, I will.'

William returned to the table, and sat down. He lifted his gaze to meet Brother Cormac's eyes, which regarded him ruefully, but without apology. Watching the two of them, John remembered with a smile the comment about scary eyes, and reflected that his monastery did seem to attract them.

'I'll not sell them, I'll not keep them, I'll not kill them. I'll set them free to take their chances in the woods,' said William.

'Oh, no,' John demurred, moving his hand in remonstrance. 'That's not prudent. You have to eat. Sell them all if you can't face the slaughter. If they run wild, all that will happen is someone will capture them and take them for their own to slaughter. You know that well. Don't listen to him, for heaven's sake – none of the rest of us do. If Brother Cormac preached the gospel with the conviction that he defends the beasts of farm and field, all

Yorkshire would have been converted by now. Leave it, William. Don't make rash promises. Bear in mind you have a wife to go home to with opinions quite as settled as any Brother Cormac may hold. Now, if you've finished upsetting each other, the both of you, and throwing up, there was something I was hoping to bring your minds to before Compline. May I do that now?'

Seeing he had their attention, John continued: 'I have been immeasurably grateful for William coming to help us keep to the strait and narrow in our accounting during this time after Brother Ambrose's death, God rest him. But we do have to find a new cellarer. I will confess frankly that while I may be called to serve as abbot of this community, in some ways I fill the office very inadequately indeed. That I have been so improvident as to allow us to reach a situation where we have no cellarer and none in training is a profound embarrassment to me, and a clear instance of that inadequacy. But 'tis where we find ourselves, and I must make the best of it. Thank God William was kind enough to come to our aid.'

He paused. Abbot John did not find it easy to admit incompetence or insufficiency. He had to humble himself considerably to make this admission. As he spoke, he kept his gaze fixed steadfastly on the edge of the table. William and Brother Cormac listened to him with sympathy, the confession of personal inadequacy being a feeling all too familiar to them both.

'Don't be too harsh with yourself,' said William. 'After all, you thought you *did* have a cellarer to replace Brother Ambrose until your replacement thoughtlessly mucked up that plan. And it's barely two years that you've had to get things in order after a long spell with no abbot here at all. Looking back over those two years, I should say you've had quite a plateful. It certainly felt like it to me. You're doing a grand job.'

John glanced at William with a quick smile, grateful for the comfort of this reassurance.

'Thank you. You might be surprised to know what an encouragement it is to hear somebody say so. Anyway, never mind that – it's the urgent need for a new cellarer I wanted to talk about. William and I have discussed this, Brother Cormac. He advises me, and I believe he is right, that of all the brothers in this community, the best man to fill this obedience would be you.'

Brother Cormac did not reply immediately, keenly aware of William and his abbot both watching carefully for his reaction. He picked up his knife from where it lay across his plate, and absently cut and poked with the tip of it the small fragments of cheese rind and bread crust that still remained there, as he thought this through.

'It's a big responsibility,' he observed quietly, after a while. 'I think I might be too impetuous, and not clever enough. What – if you don't mind my asking – what makes you think it could be entrusted to me?'

William glanced enquiringly at the abbot, who nodded to him that he might make reply to this. 'You are shrewd. You are perceptive. You are no one's fool. You are impossible to budge on any issue that matters, but you are not dogmatic. You are honest and you are not vain, not susceptible to flattery. You have been the kitchener for years, so you have a good grasp of a very vital area of the provisioning – in the infirmary and the guesthouse and the cottages, as well as in the cloister.'

Cormac nodded slowly, recognizing the truth of this. 'It feels very daunting,' he said. 'To be honest with you, I've never thought I'd work anywhere other than the kitchen and, I think you know, I've never wanted to. But... the truth of it is our kitchener is Brother Conradus, in everything but name. He is better fitted to the obedience than I have ever been. Well, Father –' he lifted his eyes to meet John's; '– if it's what you're asking of me, what can I say? I will do my best. I don't suppose it was so very easy for you to leave the infirmary work to take up the abbacy. You spoke of yourself just now as inadequate in this seat of authority. I don't see that, but if you want something to make you feel less inadequate as an abbot, me trying to be a cellarer might be just the thing. If... if I can have some guidance and counsel as I learn – especially over Easter and through all the Lady Day administration – I will serve as best I can, if you judge me fit to fulfil what will be required of me.'

'Brother Cormac?' John could see plainly Cormac's struggle to put a brave face on a sacrifice that cut very deep. His enquiry now searched direct into Cormac's soul, into old memories, allegiance, friendship, that had always been too deep-rooted to let go.

'Don't ask! Just let it be! I'll do my best. Don't dig about inside me!'

He tossed the knife down with a clatter, then reached forward and began to gather their plates into a stack, brushing the scraps from each plate together onto the top one.

'I'll take these along to the kitchen, shall I? I mean, you didn't want anything else of me?' He struggled to hold on to an attitude of submissive respect. What had been asked of him felt almost impossible to fulfil; too much responsibility and too deep a renunciation. He needed to be alone for a while to come to terms with the prospect. Understanding this, John released Cormac to go, and William opened the door for him to pass through with his accumulation of crockery all balanced on the bread board and the lantern held hanging from two fingers.

✠   ✠   ✠

'Brother? Are you... has something... what's the matter?'

Brother Conradus stopped in surprise. He held a candle to see his way, and hardly needed more than that for what he had come to do. It was not far off time for Compline. He had not expected to find anybody here.

It was dark in the kitchen. Cormac had set the lantern down along with his pile of plates and mugs and food remains, intending to sort it all out when he'd had a chance to order the muddle of his own head and heart. The austerity of the cold night air felt oddly soothing as he sat down on the scarred old stool by the huge preparation table, its surface nicked and grooved and landscaped into hills and valleys by monks and laymen chopping and scrubbing and scraping over many decades. He ran the flat of his hand slowly over the curving surface, his palm loving the contours worn by the rhythms and routines of faithful, careful, patient, daily work. 'I want to stay here,' he whispered into the cold and quiet dark. 'This is where I belong. I want to stay here.'

When they had a hustle on to get the meal ready, this kitchen could be frantic enough: but the work remained basic and simple and manual; it had nothing of the need for sophistication of mind that he imagined the work of the cellarer would involve.

There had been a night in Cormac's very early childhood when he lost everything. The black and crashing waves had flung and whirled and choked him when that ship went down. He had held on tight to his mother's unresponsive body until they succeeded in prising him off it on the shore. He had no clear memory of the event, but he remembered the feeling, and he hated the things that brought it back to the surface. He needed the safety and protection of practical and mundane daily routine. He felt his soul holding on tight to it now, in obdurate determination; and he knew that prising it off to face the turn his life had taken would be a costly business.

Brother Conradus's solemn profession at Epiphany had freed him from the daily routine of novitiate study and given him a greater scope to attend to his *Opus Dei* in the kitchen. It did not in the least surprise Brother Cormac to see him appear even at this late hour, carrying a candle and intent upon some culinary detail left unfinished.

He remembered Brother Conradus surging triumphant into the kitchen last spring, his eyes shining with satisfaction and his hands full of great bundles of ramsons that he had scrambled down the steep banks of the beck's higher reaches to pick. He had given up his siesta time to accomplish that, determined on finding them growing somewhere. Standing there with the aromatic bunches of fresh-picked leaves crammed in his hands he had told Brother Cormac that his mother said ramsons were good for the gut and against wind, good for the blood and against chills and skin breakouts – good for absolutely everything. He had noticed the year before, his first year in community before he was let loose on the kitchen, that the brothers had no ramsons chopped into their salad in the spring; and he thought that was a pity.

This year, released from novitiate obligations, it had been dandelions as well. A few fleeting days of sunshine had encouraged the hedgerow herbs, and everywhere showed an optimistic smattering of new growth. Accordingly Brother Conradus had used his precious afternoon hour every day that week to hunt for baby dandelion leaves and the first of the nettle shoots. If you picked the dandelions when they were tiny, *really* tiny (he had enthused to Brother Cormac), they had a sweetness that equalled their bitterness ('Here – try one, brother!' It was true), and added a delectable piquancy to any salad. Just two weeks later they would be their usual bitter selves, nutritious and perfectly useable, but not the same.

Brother Cormac worked faithfully and conscientiously. He did his best and experience had brought his efforts to a satisfactory and workmanlike level; but nothing in him came anywhere near Brother Conradus's single-minded devotion to raising the standards of the abbey mealtime fare from the adequate to the sublime – within the budget the cellarer set him and without offending against holy simplicity and humility.

Conradus trod quietly into the kitchen now, carrying his candle, to knead the bread dough he had set ready in the bowl just before suppertime. He had left the yeast growing, feeding on its honey, and the flour all ready with chopped herbs and salt mixed in, a cloth over the bowl; and the cruse of oil standing near the dying fire. It would be ready to mix, and Conradus knew that if he kneaded it now, oiled the lump of dough and left it wrapped in a wet cloth in the cold kitchen overnight, by the morning it would be perfectly risen. He could knock it back and leave it to prove near the bread-oven then while he lit the fire and took it up to heat, and the result would be far superior to loaves made in a hurry from dough with the main rising forced by over-proximity to the fire. But he had not expected to find Brother Cormac sitting by the table, radiating sadness and loneliness as the lantern gave off light.

'Brother? Are you... has something... what's the matter?'

Cormac looked as though his face had been carved in stone. Brother Conradus judged this could be a long, slow conversation, and he would have no second chance with his yeast once the warmth had gone off the stones of the fireplace. So he carried the things he had set ready to the table where Cormac sat brooding, and began to make his bread sponge, observing a respectful distance in his choice of location, but standing near enough to hear if Brother Cormac spoke low.

Cormac knew he should be scraping off the food remains into the bucket of waste, and at least setting the dirty dishes to soak in some hot water dipped from the big water kettle that stood comfortably on the last red embers. He couldn't be bothered. He watched Brother Conradus, the candlelight making a gentle portrait of his plump, kind face, his capable hands steadily and rhythmically kneading the dough, a focus of human sanity and purpose salvaged from the shadows of the gathering dark. Cormac's own light sat among the dirty, discarded dishes where he had left it.

'Everything seems so pointless, sometimes,' he said. 'Like you try and try, but nothing you can build ever comes to anything. Nothing is ever good enough, nothing lasts, nothing is ever your own, nothing succeeds. And after enough empty effort and years have trailed by, your teeth fall out and your eyesight goes, your limbs lose their strength and your hair falls out, you have your food mashed for you and someone steadies your hand on the cup. And then in a sallow bag of wrinkled skin, whatever you had slips out of your fingers and it all runs into the sand. Like the drifting smoke that's left when you blow out a candle. That's all it is.'

Conradus did not reply, but he almost stopped breathing as he kneaded his dough. An aspect of solemn profession that had taken him by surprise and enchanted him entirely was being taken into the confidence of the other fully professed monks. As a novice he had known, he had felt, the sense of only partial trust, the oddly marginal world of the novitiate – a monk but not a monk. And he had looked forward to the day when he took his solemn vows, became fully and properly and for real a Benedictine. But it had never occurred to him how much more vivid his brothers in community would become once they trusted him because he was one of them. As a novice working alongside Brother Cormac, Conradus had found him friendly and relaxed – Cormac's style was informal on every occasion from doling out pottage to taking his place in the sacred eucharistic rituals of Easter morning High Mass. Conradus had never found him aloof or distant. But listening to him now, he felt this moment as the deepest privilege, because he realized that Cormac had never, ever discussed his feelings about anything with him before. Not once. This precious trust came with solemn profession. Brother Conradus thought this discovery so wonderful that he became completely enthralled by the idea; the reality of whatever was happening in Cormac's life receded into the vagueness of the shadows. He kneaded the dough in silence, amazed at the privilege of trust that had come to him, rapt in the treasure of it, saying nothing at all.

Then eventually, glancing up, Conradus said: 'Did you know, I used to be so scared of you?'

Cormac blinked.

'Scared of... what? Scared of *me*? Whatever for?'

Conradus smiled; yes, it seemed so silly now. 'You were in charge,' he admitted softly. 'And I was only a novice.'

Cormac shrugged, nonplussed. 'Well... it passes...' he said. 'Look – d'you mind if I leave the dishes and all that mess until the morning?' Conradus, further surprised by Cormac's asking his permission in this way instead of telling him to wash the dishes or merely commenting that he would be leaving them, felt further overwhelmed by this sense of equality – real brotherhood.

'Of *course* you can leave them, brother!' he exclaimed, his voice full of warm emotion.

Cormac looked at him, slightly taken aback by the fulsome tone of Conradus's response.

'Thanks,' he said. 'Well... I'll be getting along then. I guess it's nearly time for chapel. You... you do a good job here, brother. This work is in good hands.'

Conradus beamed at him. Then as Cormac slipped out of the small scope of the light of candle, lantern and embers, into the darkness of the doorway, it suddenly dawned on Brother Conradus that something was very wrong, and he had been so taken up with his own inner world that he'd never even thought to ask what. Horrified at his selfishness, his heartless self-absorption, Conradus half thought to abandon the batch of dough, snatch up the lantern and run after his brother. In his imagination he actually did it. But common sense prevailed. The entire community would need good bread properly and attentively made, to enjoy a satisfying breakfast. He continued kneading until the dough came up supple and silky, then dipped a clean cloth in the kettle of water and wrung out the drips onto the stone flags of the floor. With practised hands he wiped a light coating of olive oil all over the big, soft lump of dough, swaddled it in the warm, wet cloth, and left it in the great bread bowl to rise, well away from the warmth of the dying fire, in the cool of the night. He took the dipper and scooped out some water to wash his hands free of all clinging remnants of flour and then scrubbed down the board. He glanced at the dishes Cormac had brought across from the abbot's lodging, wondering if he should tackle them tonight, but felt relieved to hear the first tolling of the Compline bell. That would have to wait until the morning, then. He took off his apron and hung it up. They were in silence now. He blew out both candles, hanging the lantern Cormac had left back on the forged hook nailed to the wall, where it belonged, and set off for chapel. As he joined the rest of the community making their way into the choir, he wondered what had been troubling Brother Cormac. He had seemed so very sad tonight.

Chapter Five

William gave the palfrey's flank an affectionate slap, wished his wife Godspeed, and stood back to watch her ride out. He took in her merry smile as she looked back and waved to him, and could not help noticing she seemed in brighter mood than she had for some time. He was not sure why. She loved her brother, he knew, and it would gladden her heart to see him and all the brothers at St Alcuin's. She had been used to freedom and independence before she married, and taking off for a few days on her own probably felt like a joyous adventure. And through the winter, life had been much confined to indoors by wet and cold. This morning, for an hour or two at least, the sun shone: it was a good day for a ride up into the hills. What nagged at him, and he would not even look at it in case it might be true, was the fear that his company did not satisfy her; that she found him oppressive and felt weary of being with him, beset as he was with so many ghouls of memory, so much baggage from the past. Maybe something healthy in her tugged to be free.

He closed the gate and lifted over the iron latch that pivoted from one side to fasten the other. Madeleine had worked hard to see that she left everything neat and in good order, nothing for him to worry about. He felt sure that in a few minutes he would think of something to do, but just at that moment a wash of sadness seeped cold through his soul, and he stood quite still. Love, he thought, turned out to be a wonderful thing that brought a man fully alive; but astonishingly painful at times.

She had left bread dough to rise, and instructions as to its baking, which she had made him repeat. He supposed that learning to make himself a loaf might be a constructive way to spend a morning. He entered their house, resolutely refusing to consider the emptiness of absence he felt there. He took the cloth from the dough, trying to remember how long ago she had left it. 'Doubled in size,' she'd said it must be. William wondered how anyone could gauge that. It grew gradually. Had it finished? How big had it been before? He saw that she had left ready the bundle of dry sticks she'd told him would be needed to heat the oven. 'Nothing is hotter than a fire of sticks,' she'd said, 'and you do have to get it really hot.' William felt ashamed to admit even to himself that he had not the least idea how to ascertain how hot was really hot, so that he'd know when the oven was right for the dough to go in. 'Make a little flour paste to seal it,' she'd said. That didn't sound too complicated anyway. He rolled up his sleeves.

✠ ✠ ✠

The rain came on when she had still three miles to cover. It came down hard and persistent. By the time she reached the abbey, she was sodden and shivering. Brother Martin opened the gate for her to ride in, and hitched the palfrey to one of the iron rings fixed into the wall of the sheltered gatehouse entrance. He lifted down her saddle packs, and grinned at her cheerfully.

'Leave your mount here, Mistress Hazell, and I'll ask Brother Peter to give her a rub down and settle her in the stable. I'll bring these across to the guesthouse for you – if what's in your pack is as wet as what you have on, come and rummage in the almonry trunks, I expect we have something no worse than damp. By heaven, that was some cloudburst, was it not! Still,

149

Brother Dominic has a fire going, I should think, so you can stand and steam and warm yourself up a little. A hot drink and a hot meal and you'll begin to feel more like yourself. Father John's expecting you, is he?'

Grateful for the kindly welcome, Madeleine lengthened her stride to keep pace with him as he hastened through the rain to the guesthouse.

'I think so,' she answered him. 'I came up just because I missed you all – he knew I would be coming sometime soon, but I didn't say exactly today. I haven't written to… to Father John.' She felt she must make an effort to let go of her habit of clinging to her brother's baptismal name, Adam. She supposed it might be more respectful to his choices in life and his status to call him John, his name in religion, especially now he was an abbot.

'If he's too busy I shall understand,' she said; 'but if he has any time to see me I'll be so grateful.'

Brother Martin gave her into the care of Brother Dominic at the guesthouse, promising to bring her word of John's whereabouts and availability once he had her horse stabled and had chance to send someone over to the abbot's house to check.

'Mistress Hazell,' he had called her, through force of habit: but Brother Martin recognized the grey palfrey as William's. So did Brother Peter when he led the horse away to the stables. Neither one of them commented to the other, but it answered a question that had lingered in the minds of them both. It had indeed been no coincidence, then, that William de Bulmer and Mistress Hazell had left one upon the heels of the other. It was a grave thing indeed for a man to break his vows like that. Even so God, and not his brothers, would be his judge. Both Brother Martin and Brother Peter had been a long while in monastic life; they turned away reflexively from both speculation and condemnation. Mistress Hazell – or would it be Goodwife de Bulmer now? – was still their abbot's family; and they would always welcome her.

Brother Dominic's cheerful smile warmed Madeleine's heart. It felt good to be here. He held the door open and welcomed her out of the wind into the warmth, taking her bags from Brother Martin with a nod of thanks.

'Hang that on the pegs here, where it has some hope of drying,' he said as she unclasped her cloak and swung it off her shoulders. 'And put your shoes on the hearth – there, that's better! If I light you a candle from the fire here, there's the makings of a fire in the chamber upstairs – go right ahead and light it, for I'm thinking you'll be wanting to spread your bits and pieces out to air. Let me take these up for you, and I'll put some soup on to heat up. You chose your time well! A week later and we'd have been into Lent, and you know our starvation rations are a marvel to behold even with the best efforts of Brother Conradus – we do well to keep body and soul together! But this week we're eating up all the left-overs of eggs and butter and such, and no pilgrims here just yet. I think I can promise you a quiet stay and a good supper!'

Madeleine separated the bundles containing gifts for the brothers from her bag of clothes, leaving the gifts on the table and following Brother Dominic upstairs. She felt comforted and lifted by his welcome. The memory of the home she had left flashed back into her imagination: William's face, so often tense and defensive, and the endless arguments that rose like marsh gas out of nowhere. She put it from her. It felt good indeed to be here, though a wave of anxiety flooded through her as she wondered if he would remember to shut up the hens, and not to strip Marigold's udder out when he was milking but let her finish drying off in time for her kid to be born and not let the milk supply build again; and if he would think to check at midday that the beasts hadn't run short of water. Resolutely she shut her home out of her mind. She had come to see her brother, and she meant to enjoy her visit.

Her clothes in the bag felt damp and looked crumpled. She thought it unwise to light and leave the fire in the chamber – she would light it later, when she settled down for the night. So she snuffed out the candle. Little sunshine broke through the clouds this day, but still she had enough light to see. Though her cloak had been wet through, she judged her dress still wearable, and her body heat should assuredly dry it better than it would dry on its own. She contented herself with spreading the garments from her pack – nothing much: a spare woollen chemise and kirtle and kerchief, woollen hose, a warm shawl and a net for her hair. She left the bag and her comb there with them, but kept her small store of money with her in the neat leather purse hung from the pretty girdle she had woven herself. On second thoughts she decided her spare kerchief felt drier than the one she wore, so she took off the blue linen one she had on and spread it out over the foot of the bed. She knotted in place her new cream-coloured kerchief woven of the softest unplyed yarn, picked up the extinguished candle and her shawl, and hastened back down the staircase to the hall below. As she reached the bottom step, she saw her brother sitting on a stool by the hearth, peacefully watching the flames and chatting with Brother Dominic as he waited for her.

'No soup, I fear, Mistress Hazell!' Brother Dominic moved forward to greet her. 'Our abbot says you're to sup with him. Never mind. We'll feed you up at breakfast!'

Madeleine smiled at him. *Mistress Hazell.* She wondered whether to correct it, and thought it might create awkwardness. She knew if she just left it, that word of her new status would find its oblique and mysterious way round the community as unobtrusively as a wisp of smoke. Before she went home most of the brothers would know exactly whose name she now bore. So she let it lie, and just smiled, and gave him back the candle. Neither did her brother make any comment on the mistake, though she felt sure it would not have gone unnoticed. He stood up to greet her, and as he enveloped her in the affection of his embrace, she knew without doubt this visit would do her good.

'Have you had a chance to make yourself comfortable?' he asked her. 'Will you come across to Vespers and then to my house for supper? I have no other guests, I was intending to eat in the frater – you've picked a good time to come.'

Happily, Madeleine walked across the familiar ground of the abbey court at her brother's side, her shawl wrapped round her against the sharp chill of the air even now the rain had eased off. They parted in the church as he went through to the choir and she took her seat in the parish benches. A feeling of such peace welled up inside her as the prayers flowed into the beautiful chanting of Mary's song – *Magnificat anima mea Dominum: et exsultavit spiritus meus in Deo, salutari meo...*

Something hard-pressed and almost exhausted in her began to relax. She had no need to fret about the horse and whether somebody had fed it. She didn't have to cook supper, or clear it away, or do the milking or feed the pig or check the hens had all come in to roost. She had nothing to do here but give herself up to the ancient heartbeat of prayer, and welcome into her soul the silent immensity of God's presence, going down to depths unimaginable, and spreading more boundless than the sweep of the sky above the moor. *Thank you...* her tired soul whispered. *Thank you...*

After Vespers, as her brother stood aside to allow her to pass before him into the abbot's lodging, she felt oddly as though here she had come home.

✠   ✠   ✠

At dusk, before the fox came prowling, William had fed the hens, counted to make sure they had both come in safely, and locked their door securely. He had milked Marigold with a sense of exultation that she trusted him these days, and would stand easy and let down her milk for him with no trouble. He took care not to strip out her udder completely, so as to gradually finish letting her dry off now she was in kid and so near her time. He filled her rack with fresh hay, and took the milk, a scant cup barely worth having these days, into the house. What remained of the morning's milk he mixed with meal and scraps for Lily the pig, keeping the new milk for his oatmeal in the morning. He took Lily her supper, tossing her half a bucket of apples he had sorted out in the store during the afternoon. They were wrinkled and their skins waxy now, but they tasted good, with an intensity of sweetness that Lily enjoyed immensely. William thought she had the worst table manners of any living being he'd ever beheld, and never liked to stay to watch her get to grips with what he brought her.

He lit the fire and investigated the bread he'd made. Madeleine had told him he would know it was cooked when it sounded hollow if he knocked it. He'd burned his fingers sealing up the oven, and had little enthusiasm for knocking on the charred crust of the loaf he brought forth an hour afterwards. Even when he did, he couldn't decide if it sounded hollow or not. And what if it didn't? He had no plans to reheat the oven and seal it up all over again.

When he broke the bread, he thought it looked passably like a loaf should look. He had followed instructions faithfully, and felt quite proud of the result. He awarded himself an achievement level halfway between Brother Cormac and Brother Conradus. Thinking of them, he wondered if Madeleine was sharing supper with John this evening. He thought she would be.

He had been glad, on his return from St Alcuin's, to find her eager to make her own visit. Something in him still felt very tender; tearing open the sac of memories and allowing them to spill out raw and bloody in John's sight had been a necessary step in the direction of sanity and peace, but it had come at a cost. John's prayer and ministry to him, receiving the eucharist at John's hands again, had reached down to the deepest place of his soul. One day he would tell Madeleine all that had happened to him, and the healing it had brought; but it felt too private even to mention just now. He wanted to be alone for a while, and reflect on who he was – and why. Her journey up to the moors came gratefully just now. But he missed her badly, even so, in the house all by himself.

When he went to bed, he looked for her shawl, the light summer one she had left behind, and wrapped it round his shoulders, telling himself it was too cold in the bed on his own. He fingered the wool of it, and stroked it against his face. He pulled her pillow nearer, and held it close to his body. He watched the vague shape of the moon climbing the frosty sky and thought they probably ought to clean the windows. A long time went by. He lay awake. Two nights, she had said. Only two. Or it might be three.

Unexpectedly, cold though it was, he suddenly found himself pushing back his blankets and scrambling out of the bed to kneel beside it.

'I'm sorry,' he said. Used to the rhythm and framework of monastic life, built upon the round of liturgy: Matins… Lauds… Terce… Sext… None… Vespers… Compline… without the pattern of psalmody and responsory, he had no idea how to pray. So he had not prayed, except in the jagged fragments of moments – like the evening kneeling at the hearth trying to make his fire catch, when he reached desperation, or the hungry repetition of the words of the psalm as John led him into laying his desolation at the feet of Christ the friend of man. He had not the first idea how to pray with Madeleine, or even suggest it to her. If he had asked her and she said yes, he would not have been sure what they would do. They attended Mass on Sundays, and sometimes she sat with the beads of her rosary slipping peaceful through her fingers in a winter evening. And that had been where it began and ended. He could not imagine how he would go about telling her of the way John had prayed for and ministered to him – the eucharist, the exorcism and blessing – not because he thought she would not understand, but because the experience had gone so deep into him that he thought uncovering it would be excruciating. It was simply too personal to put into words, to tell anybody, even Madeleine. He half wished John would tell her during her stay at the abbey – but knew he would not; John would never betray his confidence in that way.

'I'm sorry,' he whispered now. 'I haven't… I'm sorry… I just need thee to help me. I can't do this by myself. I'm out of my depth. This woman thou hast given me… she doesn't think like me. I love her… I love her so much it hurts… Help me. Please help me. I have no idea what I'm hoping thou'lt do, but I think without thy help I'm sunk. I'm not very good at marriage. Please do something. Please come and do this with us.'

The silence of the night wrapped all around him. He lingered a few minutes more, kneeling in the patch of light the moon flung across their bed; and then he crept back in under the blankets, shivering. He fell asleep; and that night, for once, the dreams that he dodged and dreaded did not come.

☩   ☩   ☩

'I'm not sure if this will work or not.'

The hesitancy in her brother's voice intrigued Madeleine. As a boy and a young man, he had been boldly assertive; not arrogant or dominating, but always decisive and quick to move from thought to action. And easily irritated, she recalled. Through his adult life she had seen little of him, just brief visits with her mother from time to time. Even when she had come to live in the abbey close at St Alcuin's after her mother's death, he had been heavily preoccupied with his new duties as abbot, and her shelter under his protection had involved little personal interaction.

When she had shared supper with him the night before, she had asked if he had the time to offer her his pastoral counsel. 'I have no one else to ask,' she had said; 'at least, nobody who would understand.'

He had looked surprised, and his voice when he agreed held a note of caution. They sat now, just the two of them, beside a fire Brother Thomas had lit for them, in the small parlour built adjacent to the abbot's lodging with one door into the cloister and one into the abbey court.

Father Theodore had been Madeleine's confessor when she lived at the abbey, and she felt unsure whether that pastoral relationship continued or needed to be re-established; it had been more than a year since she moved away, and she had not been back again since. She suspected John might prefer that she restrict any personal confidences to his hearing alone. The situation remained delicate. William had found a friendly welcome, it appeared, but nonetheless it seemed unlikely that his status as a married man should be discussed too openly or freely here. So she had asked John, not Theodore, for his time and his counsel.

'It might not work? How so? What do you mean?' she demanded now. He smiled. His sister's blunt and forthright manner had been nothing softened, he saw.

'You said you wanted to talk about your marriage to William. As far as it goes, I am willing to listen, and to offer what I can. But what do I know of marriage? And there is a familiarity between us because you are my sister that may prove to override respect. To you I am only Adam, your brother, and if my insights do not find favour I think you may scorn and dismiss them. You are not under obedience to me, nor do I suppose you look up to me. So any counsel of mine may be substantially diminished in usefulness. That's all. But we can try.'

Madeleine regarded him with curiosity. He spoke gently, and she heard humility in his voice, but he sounded sure of what he said. She thought he was looking for neither reassurance nor approval; just explaining his misgivings, with no attachment to any possible outcome. 'Thank you,' she answered him. 'I would like to try. I think William and I are at something of an impasse, and I cannot see how to go forward.'

She noted the relief in his face as she hastened to add: 'We do love each other. And you need not fear I am about to regale you with stories of what passes in our bedchamber. We have no difficulty there.'

John smiled. 'It has surprised me that some folk do indeed come to discuss such things with the abbot of a monastery – how on earth they think I know what they should be doing escapes me. I don't mind, and it's been a curious thing how the ordinary business of living together in community has application to just about any human relationship. Even so, I think being privy to the intimacy you share with William would feel a little closer to home than I'd have been comfortable with. What's been the trouble, then, if it's not that?'

'Has he never spoken to you at all about our life together?'

John's eyebrows rose. 'Do you think I would share his confidences with you if he had? Yes, he has told me a little. I think I can say as much as this: he feels he makes a rotten husband. Is that right? Do you think so too?'

'Me?' Taken aback, Madeleine blinked and considered this. John noticed she had no immediate instinct to leap to her man's defence. He waited while she gathered her thoughts into a response.

'He's… well, it's an odd thing living with someone who was thirty years in the cloister.'

John nodded. 'I can imagine there would be big adjustments to make. What kind of thing do you mean?'

Madeleine turned this question over in her mind. 'He's very quiet,' she volunteered.

'He doesn't say much, you mean?'

'Oh no, he has an opinion on everything, usually decided and stubbornly held – I didn't mean that. It's that he goes about things with barely any sound at all. When he eats his pottage, he doesn't suck it in with a great slurp and let his breath out after in a satisfied "aahhh!" like most men. When he blows his nose, he doesn't make me jump out of my skin with a wild trumpeting like a beast of the forest caught in a trap. When he hefts a bale of hay, he doesn't grunt and gasp and groan even if it's heavy – he just picks it up. When he's splitting logs the axe makes a noise, but William doesn't. I hear the crack of the wood divide and the thud of wood falling, but no loud grunting signalling to the neighbourhood that a man's making a serious effort here. He doesn't draw attention to himself at all. In the outhouse, in – maybe I shouldn't say this – in our bed; everywhere you'd expect a continuous stream of human sounds to let you know what's going on with him, there is quietness. In that respect, if no other, it's much like living with another woman – and candidly I have found that to be a relief.'

She glanced at her brother and saw the interest and amusement in his face at her description. He could imagine this very easily.

'I should think Father Theodore would rejoice if he could produce the same result in his novices! So – the quietness is not the problem, I presume?'

'No… it's… we… Well, what usually sets things off is when I run out of patience with him when he does – or says – something stupid, and then I get a bit sharp with him and he either bites my head off in his turn or else he looks completely bewildered and simply can't see my point of view. Either that or he won't talk about it at all and tells me to shut up because he says he hates arguments and just wants a peaceful life.'

John took this in, his face thoughtful.

'I've never heard William say anything stupid,' he commented eventually. 'He always seemed to be a remarkably intelligent man to me.'

A short laugh of derision escaped his sister. 'What passes for intelligence in a monastery where other men do all the gardening and thatching, the cooking and the repairs, tend the animals, sweep and scrub, make the soap and the ink, may look a lot like stupidity in a homestead.'

John nodded. 'Yes,' he said softly, 'he took a lot on. It was a courageous decision.'

In the silence that followed this observation, both of them looked into the flames of the fire, thinking.

'Does –'

'We –'

They both spoke at once, and both stopped. John gestured to his sister to continue.

'We argue all the time,' she said. 'Every day. All the time. We argue. And I'm sick of it, and so is he. I just wondered if you could help us. Mother and I didn't argue. I get the impression from what he says that William isn't used to constant wrangling either. I thought you might be able… I don't know…'

'Yes, I can help with that,' her brother answered. Madeleine thought he sounded quite certain, more confident than she had feared might be the case. She glanced at him, hopeful and expectant.

'Can you sit through a bit of an abbot's chapter, d'you think? Are you prepared for a homily of sorts?'

As he grinned at her ruefully, she could still see the boy he had been. It occurred to her for the first time that this opportunity was a privilege. To be the sister of someone wise enough and mature enough to be elected abbot of his community was a precious thing. 'I'm listening,' she said, entirely seriously. He took a deep breath.

'I've never been a married man. That's the first thing. So I might have got this completely wrong and, if I have, I can only ask you to forgive me. With that in mind, here goes.

'Please – tell me if I am meddling too far – you speak of constant wrangling; William... you said you have no difficulty, but... he is... he is not... rough with you? Not demanding? He is considerate?'

Madeleine looked at her brother, intrigued. He was blushing.

'Oh!' She understood what he meant. 'In our knowledge of each other as husband and wife? Rough? Oh – no, no! William is surpassing gentle and most tender. In fact he says, as a kind of watchword, "Patient and tender, light and slow." And he tells me – I know not what to make of this – that old Mother Cottingham told him that, and a great many other things of the courtesies between women and men too. I hardly know whether to believe him! Can you imagine such conversation between them? And he then a brother of this house! Anyway, that's what he says; and for sure he knows how to woo and win and... er... bless a woman, and goodness knows how he learned the arts of love if she did not tell him.'

'By this time, my sister, I cannot think you could tell me anything about William that would seem beyond believing. He was her confessor. Goodness only knows what they talked about! I'm glad he has found some way to put it to good use! And relieved to hear that some of the cruelties that have been visited relentlessly upon him have not bent his temperament to any kind of insensibility. Thank you. That's a burden off my mind. Let's put that to one side, then.

'So, if it's in your conversation and sharing of household tasks that contention arises, it will help if you keep in mind what he has been and where he has come from. Before he came here he was superior of an Augustinian priory of real substance. That is... I hardly like to say this, lest I myself seem to be full of self-importance, but it's a status of high degree and considerable consequence, as you must surely know. He was a man of significance and immense authority. He was not loved, it is true, but he wielded great power. In seeking sanctuary with us he had to humble himself more than I would have believed possible – and he did it magnificently. And now to leave the whole network of structures by which his life has operated and take his chances on his own with you, at his time of life – well that's magnificent too, in a crazy way. The monastic Rule has been his protective shell all his life, and he has laid it aside for you. I tell you straight, I had my misgivings about the decision, but by nothing would he be dissuaded. To be with you meant everything to him.

'Then there's another thing about William, which I imagine you have discovered by now: he has had his demons. I spoke of cruelty visited upon him, just now; he has told me something of what those who had the care of him when he was a child did to him, I have seen with my own eyes the scars on his body, and I have noted his mistrust of the bulk of humankind. The door to his heart has had rusty hinges, and not even those few of us who have been entrusted with his love find him the most uncomplicated of companions.

'But he has great strength of purpose and a quiet eye for travelling in the direction he's chosen. He is also loyal and – whatever you may think – he has a keen mind, with the wit to find his way out of almost any of the traps he has fallen into.

'But look, William aside, there are some constant features of living together in peace that I am thinking must be true for a man and wife as well as for a monastic community. Here in the abbey we are only human too, and all human beings argue. We – in community – have two big safeguards against the contention and bickering that afflict every group of people who try to live together. One is silence and the other is obedience.

'Our blessed father Benedict laid down that we enter silence after Compline and don't come out of it again until the morrow Mass is said. People take that sometimes for a purely religious discipline to encourage private prayer and reflection, and it does hone our spiritual practice, of course. But I think primarily it was put in place as a practical measure to safeguard community, because the two main danger times for antagonism are when we get too tired to be bothered with patience, and when we've just got up in the morning and haven't had breakfast yet. Benedict did away at one stroke with those daily pitfalls by instituting silence from before we were too tired to be rational until after we'd properly woken up and had something to eat. In a family household I guess it can't work in the same way, but you can follow the same principle: when you're tired or hungry – don't be drawn. Keep it sweet, keep it simple, keep it short.

'Silence supports community peace on the one hand, and obedience supports it on the other. What obedience boils down to under this roof is that I'm the abbot so the brothers have to do what I say. But *because* they have to do what I say, I have to be very, very careful what I ask them to do. They are in my hands. If I become capricious and demanding and fall in love with my own power, the community will rot from the core. Our vowed obedience puts a responsibility on me as well as them. The brothers depend on me to be humble and gentle and understanding because my word is their law; and I depend on them to be loving and patient and forgiving because I often get it wrong. I can be hasty and scornful, I can be impatient and obtuse – and they just have to bear it respectfully, because I'm the abbot. But it's an obedience of love, so they don't just take it with their teeth gritted; they accept it with humility and compassion. They know I'm doing my best. They know when I come out the other side of my bad mood I'll be ashamed of myself. They have to trust me, and I have to trust them, and that's what the obedience means – it's putting ourselves into each other's hands, deliberately making ourselves vulnerable, making our daily life into a gift to one another. It takes a whole community for a man to be an abbot.

'Let me pause there. Is that making any sense to you so far? Shall I go on? Don't worry, I'm coming to you and William in just a moment.'

He waited for her affirmation. She said nothing for a little while, then: 'That's what William does,' she said very quietly. 'What you said – deliberately making himself vulnerable. And times beyond counting he's told me that he's sorry for his shortcomings. I apologize too, but usually after him, and not as often.'

John visibly relaxed on hearing this. If she would receive what he had to say, and not resist it as a lecture or even as impertinence, he thought he had something to offer. He waited. She lifted her gaze from the flames to read his silence, and realized he was still courteously waiting for her permission to continue. 'Go on, then!' she exclaimed. He smiled.

'Well, that was the easy bit – where I'm on my own territory. Now this is where I go off the map into *Terra Ignota*, so of your charity I beg you to be patient with me. I can't look to my own experience, for I know nothing of marriage, so I'm going to look to the Scriptures, which I know I can trust.

'I'm thinking about the fifth chapter of the epistle to the Ephesians. The bridge from our life here in community to your life at home with William is in the verse that tells us to humbly give way to one another – submit to one another – in the fear of Christ. *Subiecti invicem in timore Christi*. Sister, I'm sure you must realize that doesn't mean anything like "knuckle under because you're frightened of Christ". It means that because we aspire to holiness and want to make our whole lives into a reverential space, cultivate a reverential mind, practising recollection, we maintain an attitude of humility. Are you with me?'

Madeleine understood him perfectly, but she wondered where in the passing of time the teasing urchin she had played with by the streams and on the moors had grown up into this. 'Yes,' she said. 'Go on.'

He looked at her, his lips parted in uncertainty.

'I'm listening, Adam,' she reassured him. 'You don't need to keep checking.'

He nodded, with a smile at the unintentional asperity. 'All right. Then this is where the apostle comes to teach about husbands and wives. He takes as the model for marriage the relationship between our Lord and the church – because we think of the church as the Bride of Christ. Gazing on that relationship, he sees that our Lord has suffered and died for the church, stopped at nothing in the self-giving of his love. And he sees that the church is the community of people who call him Lord, who give their lives in his service. So the model is of a relationship in which neither party has held back anything; each has surrendered all they have to the other. Each gives their whole life in order that they might be made one. This is a picture of absolute trust and vulnerability: Christ pinned helpless to the cross in love of his Bride, and the church kneeling in submission to his lordship. Do marriage like that, the apostle says. Wives, love your husbands like the church loves Christ, offering your very *lives* in submission to your menfolk. Husbands, love your wives like Christ loves the church, holding back nothing, suffering everything, laying down all you have because you love her so much.

'Now then, this is a beautiful picture, we can all see that. As a picture it works wonderfully. Where it all comes unstuck is when real people really try to do it. Then, without fail, the same old problem crops up: who's going first? Human beings are scared of being trampled. When it comes to actual flesh-and-blood mortal beings, not one of us wants to put up our hand to take the risk of doing our part of the bargain until we've satisfied ourselves that the other half is on the table first. So we never begin. Do you see?

'Actually… in your marriage to William – dear sister, don't be hurt or take offence, bear with me – I can see him struggling to do his part, but I can't see you doing yours as well as you might.

He's a proud man, and used not only to absolute governance but also to admirable competence. To set that aside and let himself look foolish and inept will be completely crucifying to a man like William de Bulmer; but he thinks you're worth it.

'What he needs from you is what the brothers here in their charity and humility give me: obedience. Not to him, I mean, but to Christ; just as in their vow of obedience to the abbot, the way the brothers here are taking is not obedience to *me*, John Hazell, but to Christ. Sister, William needs you to trust him enough to submit to him, even when he isn't doing all that well. Even – indeed especially – when he's said or done something stupid, he needs you to submit to him for the sake of divine order, out of reverence for Christ.'

John looked anxiously at his sister. He could not imagine this going down well. Madeleine could not have been described as meek in any imaginable circumstance.

'So… what does that mean in practical terms, in daily life?' She frowned. Her tone of voice expressed the suspicious end of caution. 'It hasn't got to be all "Yes, William" and "No, William", "Of course, William", and waiting on him hand and foot, has it? Give me a few instances.'

John thought about that.

'Well…' he said slowly, 'let's say you were out at the market all day and when you got home it turned out he forgot to shut the hens in and as a result a fox had caused mayhem and you'd lost half the flock. Might that happen?'

Astonished, his sister searched his face. 'Has he spoken to you about that?'

John grinned. 'Oh. I see. It did happen. No, he never told me so. Still, it makes a good example then! Well, "in the flesh" as the apostle would say, if a man did such a thing his wife would go beserk and think she had every good reason to do so. She'd call him every name she could think of and pour indignation on his head until boiling pitch began to look like a merciful alternative. She'd scold him until he felt completely humiliated, and he'd go to bed scowled at and unkissed and lie awake in the moonlight trying in vain to think of some way of making amends.

'But the apostle is saying that's not how we do it under Christ. That's because Christ really sees us, with the insight of love. Christ is quick to compassion, and knows full well the man is more ashamed of himself than he can bear already. In marriage as the apostle imagines it, the wife offers not a word or look of reproach. She accepts that accidents happen. Her love is magnanimous and generous. She hooks up the dead birds quietly, out of sight. As she spins at the fireside that night, maybe she seems a wee bit quieter than usual – that would be because through gritted teeth she is silently praying: "O Fountain of Wisdom, thou hast saddled me with this dolt, this nincompoop, this addle-brain: right then, give me the grace not to kill him!" But she takes it to God and she leaves it with God. She offers her husband no reproach, because she is submitted to him.

'But then let's suppose this is all too much for the wife. She comes home, she finds the hens dead and dying, and she lets rip like thunder and lightning. What's her husband to do? Well, "in the flesh" as St Paul has it, he might go on the defensive. Where was she all day anyway? What did she mean by coming home so late? Aren't they her dratted poultry in the first place? How much is it going to cost to replace them? This will be the last time she goes to market if that's where it's all going to end up. He might even hit her, if her scolding winds him up past what he can bear.

'But the Scripture teaching says no, don't do it like that. Submit to one another. Love her like Christ loves the church. If she wants to hammer nails in, lie there and take it. If she's minded to jam a cap of thorns on your head, bite your lip and wipe the blood out of your eyes. Keep your eyes fixed on one thing and one thing only: letting nothing – but nothing – sour the sweetness of love.

Let it hurt you, let it shame you, let it lacerate you; but don't let it stop you loving her.

'Have I exhausted your patience? Have I said enough for now?'

Madeleine was sitting very still, her face brooding. 'Go on,' she answered him.

'Well, then: this thing has to be mutual, it has to be reciprocal to work properly, to get the result it's meant to achieve. If in our community here the brothers are humble and submissive and the abbot is arrogant and self-serving and demanding, it all starts to unravel. If the abbot is gentle and humble but the monks are proud and lazy and insubordinate, the whole thing collapses in an instant. Same in a marriage. If the woman serves her husband humbly and he thinks "Oh, good!" and sits back self-satisfied, "Wife, get me this, get me that!" then it isn't what the apostle envisaged. If the man is forbearing and gentle and the woman takes it as her opportunity to get away with being a nag and a shrew, then it's just hell on earth. It takes two.

'How do you keep your hens from roaming too far afield and roosting in the trees, Madeleine?'

'What?' Surprised by the sudden question, she turned her face to him. 'You know what I do. I clip their wings.'

'Oh. And how do you do that?'

'What are you talking about? You know perfectly well how to clip a hen's wings.'

'Pretend I don't. What do I have to do?'

'You just trim the tips of the flight feathers on one wing. It unbalances them, so they can't fly.'

'Exactly so. That's why the apostle urges that in marriage a man and a woman be not unequally yoked, but be both submitted to Christ; because it takes two to make this work. Unbalanced, it can't take off, it can't fly. One of you can start the ball rolling maybe, but in the end the thing takes two. The

168

man must be as humble and vulnerable as Christ stripped naked with his arms opened wide on the cross. The woman must be as gentle and submissive as the faithful people of God kneeling in simple humility before their Lord. Madeleine, am I describing your marriage?'

No sound followed this question but the settling of slow-burning logs on the hearth as the smoke drifted peacefully up the chimney above their red glow.

'What do you think?' she asked at last, her voice low.

'I think it's a hard lesson to learn and it asks a lot of anyone. I think even when we've practised for years it takes more than most of us have, to get it right. Again and again in community here, I have to ask my brothers' forgiveness when I forget myself and say something cutting or contemptuous or intolerant. And I imagine it must be exactly the same in a marriage. Except, in the night, where we have our holy silence to help us, you married folk are also blessed with an extra way to put things right.'

She said nothing. Then she moved uneasily, her face contorted in puzzlement. 'This sounds all very attractive, but... well, in real life I can't always be stopping to think about William. There's work to be done, and only the two of us to get through it all. That's mainly where we fall out – there's so much to do, and I get exasperated with him when he forgets things and he's clumsy and slow. It's all very well for you, there's a veritable army of men here to work together; at home it's only me and William.'

John nodded. 'I know what you mean. Not all our men are equally skilled of course – if you'd ever stood and watched Brother Thomas trying to work alongside Brother Germanus you might think twice about saying it's all very well for us; but I do know what you mean.

'I understand that the work has to be accomplished – the beasts fed and the place maintained and the crops sown – of course it does, but... shaping a life as God meant it to be involves paying attention to the *way* we do things. The thing is, the journey determines the destination, if you see what I mean. The way we take is what settles the place we will arrive at. If you spend the next ten years bickering with your man and belittling him, you will be sowing the seeds for a harvest of misery in your old age. He won't leave you. William would never leave you, of that I am sure. He's no slouch – he has the most phenomenal application and tenacity. But you could lose him in other ways. He could become very bitter and withdrawn, and he is capable of great coldness. He was a ruthless man once.

'I think, if you are willing to let things go sometimes, not have to have everything done *right*, that will help. So what if the fox steals a hen or two? Is that more serious than letting the devil steal your marriage? Do you really want William dancing like a puppet while you pull the strings, afraid to offend you, frightened of what you'll say if he makes a mistake?'

He observed her quietly. 'Is that… am I being too harsh?' he asked her gently.

She shook her head. 'I think you've put your finger on it,' she replied, her voice dull and defeated. 'I'm not a very good wife at all.'

John's hand moved in a gesture of protest. 'You're the right wife for William. It's hard, in middle life, to make adjustments, is the only thing. It's the same here when older men who have been widowed feel a vocation to monastic life. But never mind that. Could you do it, do you think? Might you be able to make the choice to be kind a higher priority than being right? Could you keep your mind's eye on the way you've chosen and trust it will arrive at somewhere worthwhile?'

'Yes, but – the "way" you're talking about is only my demeanour towards my husband, which is only one part of my life. That way might arrive at a beautiful marriage, but a sloppy homestead!'

'Yes,' said John. 'So what? Anyway, it won't, it couldn't. I haven't known William de Bulmer long, but long enough to be astonished at the power of his focus on housekeeping accounts. I promise you, if he let a chicken die unbudgeted, there is no one on God's earth who would feel it more keenly than him. With or without constant scolding he'll make a fine householder in the end. He's as sharp as a honed blade and diligent with it. I think you have to trust him.'

He watched her as she weighed these words carefully, frowning in concentration.

'Has that… is that any help at all?' he asked her.

'Yes. Yes it is,' she said. She lapsed into silence again, and he waited; he did not hurry her. 'Adam, I think maybe I ought to go home,' she said at last.

Her eyes met his. *Such kindness there…* she thought.

'Madeleine, if I haven't already talked you into the ground, there is one more thing I had it in mind to tell you.'

Her eyebrows lifted in enquiry: 'Which is? Spit it out.'

John's heart gave thanks that it seemed life had left him one person at least who had no idea how to speak to an abbot. He thought it might be possible to get all too comfortable with deference and respect. He smiled at her.

'It's something I heard Father Theodore telling our novices when I sat in on his teaching circle a while ago. It made quite an impression on me, and I've borne it in mind ever since.

'He said that everything we do or say in our interactions with each other every day we should be able to sort into one of four bundles. Imagine four boxes each having a label glued on, he said. The labels on the boxes are: THANK YOU, I LOVE YOU, I ASK YOUR PARDON, and PLEASE HELP ME. So, the way we treat people, our manner towards them and the words we say, the things we do – everything about our attitude towards them should be able to be sorted into those four boxes. He said what's in those boxes would be fit to offer our brothers in community. Then he said there's a fifth box with a label crowded with crabbed script. It says something like I HATE YOU – I RESENT YOU – I'M JEALOUS OF YOU – I'M FURIOUS WITH YOU – I DON'T NEED YOUR HELP, THANKS VERY MUCH! – I DESPISE YOU – YOU GET ON MY NERVES – I CAN'T BE BOTHERED – YOU'RE A COMPLETE NIT-WIT – LEAVE ME ALONE. Theodore said anything in our lives that couldn't be sorted into those first four boxes could probably be tossed into that fifth one – and that fifth box full of these spiky, bitter, acrid herbs, we offer up to God. And he eats them. And digests them. And the divine gut turns them into what they already were all along. When they have passed through the body of God their true nature is revealed, and we don't want anything more to do with them. It was such a weird and vivid idea – I couldn't be sure if it was heresy or not, but it certainly caught the imagination of the young men in our novitiate!'

Madeleine didn't laugh. 'What were the first four boxes again?' she asked.

'Thank you, I love you, I ask your pardon, and please help me.'

She nodded. 'I can remember that. And God eats the rest. Very well; I'll try it.'

He was ready then, she could see, to draw her audience with him to a close. Tentatively, humbly, he offered to say a prayer with her, and this she accepted eagerly. She expected him to use the form of words that concluded a confession – blessing and absolving her, signing her with the cross; but instead he bent his head in quiet humility and spoke to his Lord Jesus as though Christ in his homespun robe and sandals sat there with them at the fireside, on one of the low wooden stools.

'Ah, my beloved Lord, you see how things are with us; you know the struggle and the heartache that have touched William's and Madeleine's life together. You see the love, and you feel the times they slip and fall. Help them to find the way of humility and gentleness. You who came through locked doors and stone walls to find your friends, and breathed into them your Holy Spirit, gift of peace, find your way into Caldbeck Cottage, and impart your breath of peace into the everyday life there. Help them, cheer them, encourage them, bless them, lead them, and all for your love's sake, that the peaceable kingdom of kindness may reign in their lives. Amen.'

Such a comforting sense of serenity and reassurance settled into Madeleine's heart as John spoke these words, that she hardly dared move lest she lose the loveliness and the deep sense of peace. She opened her eyes and looked into the glow of the fire. 'Amen,' she whispered. 'Amen.'

But then she knew her brother had given her as much time as he had, and she got up from her stool ready to make her farewell.

'Won't you stay with us another night?' John asked her courteously. 'You don't want to go up to the farm and see the new lambs? You are surely welcome; we'd be glad to have you here longer.'

The words lined up in her head ready to be spoken – *Adam, I'm not stupid! It's perfectly clear to me how busy you are and how many other people are waiting to call on your time. You've told me exactly what I needed to know, I got what I came for, so now I'll leave you in peace.*

She drew breath – and then she stopped. The huge grin on her brother's face as he watched her recalibrating her thought processes annoyed her intensely. With an effort, reformulating, she said: 'Thank you – that's so kind. I should have loved to stay an extra night; indeed I'd planned to, because I hadn't expected you would be able to make the time to see me right away – and brother, I am so grateful. This is such a welcoming place, so full of peace. But I also think William might be glad of...' Here she paused. *An extra pair of hands* was what she'd intended to say. She changed it. 'Glad to have me back home,' she said instead.

Speaking the words made her realize how costly is vulnerability – to admit that she was loved, and needed not just to do the chores but for herself. It surprised her how hard it was to say, how shy it made her feel. She looked up at the kindness in her brother's face. 'How'm I doing?' she asked, and he threw back his head and laughed.

'Madeleine, it's been a treat to see you! Mind you tell that man of yours I sent him my love. And yes, I'm sure you're right, he'll be missing you and it'll warm his heart to know you wanted to come home earlier than you said. He adores you, you know. He absolutely adores you.'

He opened his arms to her, and gave her a quick hug, then stepped back, ducking his head in a little bow of courtesy as he opened the door into the abbey court for her, and stood aside to let her pass through.

'I don't know if I'm going to remember everything,' she said doubtfully as they crossed the court together, 'much less manage to put it into practice.'

He shrugged. 'Your best will be good enough. And there's a short version that I personally find comes in handy.'

'Oh?' She stopped. 'What is it?'

'KYMS.'

'Which is what?'

'Keep Your Mouth Shut. When all else fails it's very useful! Now, my sister, I must leave you. It's been a blessing to have you here with us. Come back soon. Brother Martin will fortify you with some bread and soup before you set forth on your journey – but don't let him keep you gossiping. Your husband will have words to say to us if we detain you so you're still abroad when night falls!'

Chapter
Six

The joy that Madeleine had anticipated in her husband, on being surprised by her early return, was not as apparent as she had hoped and imagined. He did look surprised when he came into the small courtyard at the front of their house, alerted by the sound of the horse and the gate-latch – but he seemed guarded and even faintly defensive, rather than delighted. This irritated Madeleine. *What's the matter with you? Are you not pleased to see me? Would you prefer I go back?* She stifled these words before they had a chance to escape, and gave herself time to reframe the greeting as she slipped down from the saddle, William meanwhile courteously holding the reins for her.

'I missed you,' she said with a wide, friendly smile, leaning forward to leave a kiss on his cheek; 'and I thought you might be missing me. So I came home.'

William blinked, but did not immediately reply. 'Er… good…' he said then, cautiously. 'Well, I'm glad to see you, but… you could have… are you sure…?'

Oh, for heaven's sake! Madeleine's inner voice snapped back in impatience, exasperated at his failure to respond to her loving approach, and a little hurt by his lukewarm response. She took a deep breath. 'Well?' she smiled at him, keeping her tone teasing and playful with some effort. '*Did* you miss me?'

He looked at her, a cloud of puzzlement crossing the changeable sky of his eyes. 'Yes,' he said. 'Hang on a minute.'

He unstrapped her pack and handed it down to her, then led Nightmare away to the stable where he set out half a bucket of water and some fresh hay, took off all the trappings and rubbed down the sweaty animal. This took more than a quarter of an hour, by which time Madeleine had given up and gone indoors. He seemed, she thought, more taciturn than ever, and she began to regret having come home early. She would have loved to see the new lambs at the abbey, to have spent an hour with Brother Michael in the infirmary, to have enjoyed the peaceful luxury of drifting in the slow current of monastic worship and the pleasure of having all her meals cooked and cleared away by somebody else.

In the house she found everything tidy – careful inspection turned up no signs of anything burnt or broken. The remains of yesterday's loaf gave evidence of instructions faithfully and successfully followed. She tied her apron around her waist and cut two onions from the braided swags that hung in the scullery, taking them to the table to chop for supper. She kept her eyes on the task as she heard the latch click and the following silence that stood in for William's footfall. Then she felt him close behind her, and his hands gentle on her shoulders, turning her round to face him. *Look what you're doing! I've got a knife in my hands!* The warning rose sharp to her lips; but she didn't say it. She didn't say anything. She looked up into his face, stretched up and placed the softest of kisses on his lips.

The perplexity in his face annoyed her. But she continued to smile up at him, and still she said nothing. She let the pause extend.

'I did miss you,' he admitted then, his voice soft and tender. 'I missed you dreadfully. I curled up with a pillow, and I buried my face in your shawl, and I wanted you back here with me. Thank you for coming home. I was afraid you might have come back just for fear I'd make a mess of looking after the place without you.'

Too right! She didn't let that quip escape her mouth either. 'Sweetheart,' she said, 'you ran an Augustinian priory, you rescued a Benedictine abbey's finances: I expect you can keep an eye on our home for a while without anyone to nag you. I saw the bread you made. That looks excellent. I thought I'd make a pot of soup to go with what's left.' *Assuming as usual you couldn't be bothered to feed yourself properly at midday and contented yourself with seeing off the cheese,* her inner dialogue continued.

Quizzical, searching, William's eyes looked into hers. *What?* she thought, annoyed by the expression on his face. *Anyone would think I was never nice to you! It's not so very strange as all that, is it?*

'Thank you – thank you kindly. Yes, I'd love that. If you're sure you aren't too tired from your journey.' He sounded pleased, but more wary than ever. He kissed her, light as a stray petal landing on the ground, and released her from his embrace. He hesitated, unsure if this was the right moment to continue the day's work while the light permitted, or if he should take some time to be appropriately attentive to his wife. Hedging his bets, he thought he'd tarry a while indoors with her, then see to the animals while she finished their supper preparations. He felt embarrassed that he had done nothing about making supper himself – he had given it no thought whatever. The cheese had all gone, so he would probably have eaten a hunk of bread and dripping, a couple of apples and maybe an egg, washed down with a mug of ale at the fireside. That seemed plenty to him, but he had a feeling Madeleine would consider it a shiftless, inadequate apology for a meal. Even so, having caught him out in his feckless approach to housekeeping, she didn't seem to be cross with him. She didn't look put out at all.

As she chopped onions and garlic and herbs, Madeleine felt aware of William's eyes resting meditatively upon her; quiet, thoughtful, observant. She chatted pleasantly to him about her stay at the abbey – telling him how John had made himself available to spend time with her today, and she had shared his supper in the abbot's lodge the previous evening. William listened, his gaze watchful, penetrating; like a curious fox, she thought, or a cat intrigued by a pleasingly unfamiliar movement.

Madeleine felt a little self-conscious, as though his eyes in deliberate delicacy lifted away the layers of what she wanted him to see, and silently, persistently probed her hidden self, feeling for the truth of her, touching the contours of change and present reality. It came as a relief when, seeing their supper would shortly be done and the sinking sun had set the whole sky aflame, he went outside to feed the animals and shut them in for the night.

Maintaining careful courtesy and gentle speech began to drain Madeleine's resources after a while. She wondered if the brothers at St Alcuin's found it as hard work as this, or if it somehow came naturally to them. Even so, she had to admit, pleasant and cheerful conversation added something of a flavour of courtship to their evening together. Everything felt less empty and prosaic than it usually did. When they had eaten and cleared away the supper things, weariness descended on Madeleine; two hours on horseback and the effort of unremitting sweetness began to take their toll. They turned in early, and in the intimacy of their chamber she felt glad enough to snuggle into William's arms, at least until their body heat warmed the bedding enough to make everything cosy as she drifted off to sleep. But evidently that was not all her husband had in mind.

'If you're not too tired…' he murmured gently, kissing her brow… her cheek… with consummate tenderness.

Like a thin, snaking river of bile the words that came easy in response ran through her familiar mind: *Yes! I am way too tired! What did you expect, for heaven's sake? I've ridden all the way back from St Alcuin's and not stopped for breath before cooking your supper! Can't you just wait until tomorrow?*

She listened to the words in her head, and she thought of the brothers at the abbey, letting all the bitterness and cynicism that arose from weariness come under the kind cloak of the Grand Silence. She thought that was all very well for them; once Compline was done and dusted all they had to do was go to bed – nobody would ask anything further of them until the morning. At least – they did have to leave the warmth of their blankets in the middle of the night to pray, but perhaps they were used to that. Could they *possibly* get used to that? Or was it their gift of love, in spite of being tired, no matter what they felt like – because this was their vow, their way, their commitment? Was it meant to be something they would never get used to, to make sure this way they had chosen could not degrade into a comfortable religious routine, simply going through the motions?

So what she said to William was: 'My darling… I can't imagine being too tired to want your love.'

He made no comment, but as he held her and kissed her and caressed her, for the first time the thought came to her that this was not simply something happening between them, nor did he intend it as a demand upon her – he was giving her the very best he had to offer, doing his utmost to please her. It surprised her to find herself humbled and moved that it should be so, and further surprised her to discover that his love, tender and gentle and considerate, added no burden to her weariness but smoothed away the fractious ennui and the aches of a long day, leaving her comfortable, peaceful and contented. Later, she drifted off to sleep, still held in his arms. William, momentarily alert as he watched her eyelids drowse shut, felt vaguely unnerved by the change in his wife, and very, very grateful as he allowed himself, too, to be drawn down into slumber.

He woke, as he usually did from sheer force of habit, an hour or so after midnight and at about half-past five in the morning, well before even the first lightening of the dawn. The second time he knew he would not go back to sleep. He lay thinking and praying, turning over in his mind the difference in Madeleine after one short visit with her brother. He wondered what on earth John had said to her. He contemplated the day's tasks waiting to be done, but he didn't move, not wanting to wake her – she was sleeping so peacefully. Eventually, towards daybreak, as the darkness lifted, she stirred. William thought she must surely be awake by now.

'It's still cold,' he said conversationally, 'but –' he gave an experimental puff – 'I can't see my breath.'

Madeleine huddled down deeper under the blankets. 'Perhaps you're dead,' she mumbled sarcastically. William grinned, reassured. *That's my girl!* he thought. He took the opportunity to slide quietly out of bed and dress himself, leaving her to doze off to sleep again.

When Madeleine finally came to, she could hear from downstairs the familiar noises of logs fetched in from the store tumbling from her husband's arms into the basket, then the scratch of the flint, and the spit and crackle of the kindling wood. Next, the clatter of the chain as he lifted the porridge pot onto the hook. To these sounds of everyday was added one she did not remember hearing before: William singing – a simple lilting setting of the *Benedicite*. She lay in the warm nest of their bed and listened. *What a nice voice he has,* she thought. *Why haven't I heard it before?*

✠   ✠   ✠

After he had bidden his sister farewell, Abbot John turned his mind with reluctance to another encounter that he could no longer put off. Brother Cormac's uncomplaining acceptance of the obedience of cellarer had startled him. He had braced himself for a tussle to prise Cormac out of his niche in the kitchen. John realized that he must have underestimated him. The cost and the sacrifice, he had seen in Cormac's face all too vividly, but the resentment and stubborn protest he had anticipated had never come, and for that the abbot's heart was thankful. He had no expectation that things could go smoothly twice. He had to do something about his disastrous prior. With this in mind, he had asked Father Chad to come to his lodging after None. After the midday meal and before None, John wanted first to approach the possibility of change with Father Francis. He had hesitated over this, wishing he'd thought to seek William's counsel before his friend returned home. In principle, as abbot, he could ask anything of the monks in his community, and they were vowed to obedience. In practice, it paid to tread gently, to invite more than to command, to discuss rather than to instruct. John thought it unwise to force anybody to an obedience – that would be counter-productive. And he didn't want to end up with no prior in the same way as he had been caught on the hop with no cellarer. So he felt reluctant to lever Prior Chad out of his obedience without having ascertained for sure that someone was willing to replace him. For this reason, he wanted to sound out Father Francis first. On the other hand, he felt that in kindness, Father Chad should be the first to know his role in the community was just about to change. It seemed unfair that Francis should have known all about it beforehand.

He tried to imagine what William would say, how he might approach it – and failed completely. The embarrassment of Brother Ambrose's death having left the community with no cellarer and none in training made a difference to this decision now. The appointment of his prior was John's choice entirely; that was laid out very clearly in the Rule. In this matter he had no responsibility to consult the brethren in Chapter. But the cellarer debacle had happened, and that pushed the stakes higher. He could not afford to put a foot wrong here. A sense of stability, John knew, was an essential component of monastic contentment. The boat had been rocked too often. This was not a time to take risks. He had to keep a man in place in the essential obedience of prior – even if that man was Father Chad. So he had cautiously and uncertainly gone for the option of talking to Francis first.

They had started lambing up on the farm. Brother Thomas would be out this whole day, which presented an opportunity for a very discreet conversation with Father Francis and, if all went well, for consolidating the change with Father Chad later in the day.

John recognized an unusual fluttering of nervousness in his belly. The simple kind of personal authority in his day-to-day dealings with the men of his community came naturally to him, but faced with the bigger, more strategic decisions he felt out of his depth. He knew that he had to get this right, and he did trust William's counsel and judgment of character. He had agreed, once the idea had been suggested to him, that Francis would probably make a good prior: but he also knew that human temperament is never certain, and all he could really do was make his best guess. He would have liked a better security than that. He wondered as well, though no word had reached him, if there might be any murmurings because he had sought William's counsel rather than the feeling of the community in Chapter, in settling on Brother Cormac to fill the obedience of cellarer. In the case of finding a new prior, he couldn't have brought the matter to Chapter even if he'd wanted to, because Father Chad was very much alive and in post, and John had no wish to humiliate him; this had to happen quietly. John closed his eyes as he sat thinking, trying to see round the bends in the road that lay ahead. 'Help me,' he whispered. 'Oh, please help me. I am not man enough for the task you have entrusted to me. Help me. Put me in the way of your grace. Shine into me the insight of your wisdom. Where I am dull and obtuse, of your charity let the light of your Spirit lead me...'

The knock at his door betokened well. Firm, but not insistent. Audible but not loud. John wasted no time in answering the knock. '*Benedicite!*' he welcomed his brother as he opened the door. 'Come in!'

Brother Tom had paused to light the fire before he took off up the hill to the farm that morning, and it glowed on the hearth still. John felt torn over this. After years of working in the infirmary, kept always comfortingly warm, he felt the cold; and it had been a hard winter. He also thought it in some ways improvident to allow the wet to obtain too entrenched a hold on the monastery buildings. During his own time in the novitiate, moss and fungus had grown freely on the walls. Books, so precious and laborious in the making, went mouldy. Men coughed their way through the fogs and frosts, shivering in damp robes. John saw the sense of warmth. On the other hand he knew – and William had pointed it out – that their consumption of firewood had risen considerably since Father Peregrine's abbacy had ended and his had begun. The guilty sense of extravagance nagged at him. He tried to compromise, by permitting himself a fire, but keeping it burning low. He felt glad of it now. This large room, so airy in the summer, felt bleak indeed in February without the kindly welcome of fireglow on the hearth.

'Come – sit you down, brother,' he said to Francis, who surprised him by sitting not on the chair set ready for him, but on the stones of the hearth. Francis, sensitive to the fleeting and tacit hiatus, looked up in consternation before he had fully settled. 'Not here? I'm so sorry!' He moved at once to get up.

'No, no! Stay where you are! You're a blessing to me! Think of what you'll do for my sense of power and authority as I look down upon you from my throne!' John smiled at him, and drew one of the chairs closer to the fire to seat himself. 'If you feel chill, feed the fire. Spring's coming, I do believe, but it's still perishing cold.'

Francis realized that he had chosen this seat without thinking because, in his novitiate days, this had been where he had always sat when Father Peregrine called him into this room to talk through his progress in religious life, the unfolding of his vocation. There had been, he remembered, some painful and powerful encounters with his own soul as he sat here by the fire, allowing the gentle, persistent probing of his superior's questions to uncover aspects of himself he had struggled and failed to keep hidden. The struggles had been immense, but the prize of self-knowledge and peace and the recognition of Christ at the heart of it all had been worth the pain and turmoil. He felt a sudden shaft of sadness at the passing of those days, that relationship. Swift on its heels came the recollection that it could not be easy to follow in the tracks of Father Peregrine's sandals. Glancing up at his abbot, who sat watching him, waiting for his return from the momentary reverie, Francis felt ashamed.

'What were you thinking about?'

'I... well... it goes back years, now, doesn't it – but, when I was a novice, when I came here for audience with Father Peregrine, he would invite me to light the fire, and I would sit here on the hearth. He touched on some sore places and went with me down some dark paths.'

John nodded. He understood. He also noted the faint embarrassment, and felt grateful for Francis's sensitivity to the awkwardness of comparison.

'It's all right,' he said. 'I loved him too.' He thought it better to leave the moment and move on. This could get maudlin. 'Brother, I have something to ask of you.'

He paused. He supposed he should call Francis 'Father' really. There was something innately informal and fraternal about

Francis that made the suggestion of gravitas in the word 'Father' seem inherently unlikely. He hoped he was about to do the right thing. Francis looked not at him but into the embers of the fire, waiting with thoughtful attention for his abbot's request.

John drew breath. Was he going to do this? It would be a grave thing, to topple his prior from his seat of privilege and power. Replacing him with someone like Francis might raise some eyebrows. *William de Bulmer, I sincerely hope you're right*, John murmured in his soul. Francis felt his hesitation, and glanced up at him, curious.

An abbot's prior works very closely with him. If Francis were to fill this obedience, John would make him his confessor as well, and no serious decisions would be made without consulting him. This was part of the problem with Father Chad. The respect and strength implied in the relationship was, John had to admit, simply lacking. Apart from his esquire, placed to see his weaknesses and vulnerability more clearly than anyone, the abbot's prior came most nearly privy to his heart. John thought he might as well therefore take him into his confidence starting now.

'Father Chad is a good man but a weak prior.' He went straight to the point. 'He is prayerful and kindly, but he is not decisive, and authority sits ill on his shoulders. He has served well and faithfully in his obedience, but I think a change would bless him and bless the community. I have not yet spoken with him about this. Before I do, I wanted to ask you, Father Francis: are you willing to accept the obedience of prior in this community?'

Francis looked up at him in sheer, naked astonishment; and after one stunned moment of disbelief he began to laugh.

'*Prior*?' he said. '*Me*? You *cannot* be serious!' And John knew then, looking at Francis's flabbergasted, stupefied, shocked face, that he had asked the right man. Not a trace could he discern of ambition, or self-congratulation, or elation. Francis was simply dumbfounded.

'Well, I am,' John answered him.

'But… look… you know me. I'm a complete nitwit, always have been. I talk too much, I laugh too much, I clown around – still, even still. I'm just a lightweight, I – John, I'm *nothing*! And I'm sorry, that was disrespectful to call you just "John". You see what I mean? I'd be useless! Oh, for goodness' sake, ask somebody else!'

John nodded thoughtfully. 'Who?'

'Well… er… I don't know. What about – er – what about… er…' Francis saw the problem his abbot faced. 'There isn't really anybody, is there? To be candid with you, I don't think there's really anybody, even if you include me. Why… whatever made you think I could… ?' He shook his head, amazed.

'I didn't want this matter leaking out through the community,' said his abbot. 'So I took counsel with William de Bulmer.'

'William? William de Bulmer thought I would make a good prior? He must be off his head! Truly, Father, I'm just a birdbrain – I'd let you down, I'd be incompetent.'

'Have you finished? Is that your only objection?'

'Um… yes – well, isn't that enough?'

'Will you do it? I need your help, my brother. Will you accept this obedience?'

And John saw the incredulity fade from Francis's face, and sober consideration replace it. 'What about Father Chad? He will be hurt, surely? He will feel humiliated.'

John drew breath in a sigh. 'I will do my utmost to protect him from that. I will couch it in the best terms I know how to do. But yes, he may indeed feel debased. I will do what I can.'

'What is… can you explain to me what would be required of me? There isn't much about it in the Rule, is there? Unless I haven't been paying attention. I mean, I know what being a prior looks like from the outside, but – well, to me it just looks like Father Chad. I can't distinguish between the vocation and the man. If you were away, I know the prior would have to stand in for you, but what about when you're here?'

'You would help me with ministering all the temporal matters – help me in making decisions, in receiving guests, in writing letters and overseeing all the different areas of service in our common life. And as you rightly said, if I were away or fell ill, you would act in my stead. Unless that happened, the work is not onerous, because the responsibility rests with me.'

'But if, God forbid, it did happen – if you fell sick as Father Peregrine did – have I the stature and judgment to hold everything together?'

'Well, if you have not, at least you don't annoy everybody. Don't underestimate yourself, Father Francis – and don't underestimate the grace of God to allow you to rise to your calling. Now, enough of this shilly-shallying – will you do it?'

Francis took a deep breath. 'For you and in service of Christ, yes I will,' he answered his abbot, 'if you will promise to be patient with me, Father, and if you will guide me.'

He spoke with such unpretentious humility and looked John in the eye with such sincerity that for a moment John felt incapable of framing any kind of reply; he just thought how blessed he was to have his life shaped by a community in which the gospel had forged the lives of men on Christ's own anvil.

✠   ✠   ✠

For the first time she could remember, Madeleine woke before her man. Dawn lightened the sky and faint colour streaked the grey, but it was still before daybreak. In their chamber, the darkness had barely lifted. She lay quietly, looking at her husband's face. Curled up in sleep his chin rested on his hand, and something of the dignity and peace of his face in repose moved her deeply. Then his eyes opened and looked straight into hers.

'Good morrow, Scary-eyes,' she said.

'Oh, please!' he mumbled, and closed them again.

'Sorry,' she whispered. 'Sorry!' And she placed a soft kiss on his brow.

One of the scary eyes grudgingly re-opened. 'Is it safe to come out?'

She snuggled closer to him, and he uncurled and received her into his arms, she peaceful with her head on his breast, he silently loving her close to him there.

After a while, she spoke again. 'I don't really know how you managed not to be a complete monster,' she said.

'*What*?' She felt him move in consternation, twisting his head in an attempt to look down at her. 'Whatever brought that on? What are you talking about?'

She played absently with the hair of his beard. 'I was looking at you while you were sleeping... thinking of the things you've told me about your home and your family when you were a little lad... so frightening and cruel... It sounded as though you never knew anything else in all your childhood... and children grow into what they know... so I'm surprised you didn't turn into a monster.'

She felt him relax, and his hand gently stroked her hair as he turned these words over in his mind.

'Well...' he said eventually, 'there would be those who said I did. On that notorious occasion – you must have heard tell of it – when I received Father Columba du Fayel at our priory... St Dunstan's... um... Father Peregrine they used to call him... and he came to challenge my intentions... didn't trust me to do anything good... I gave him a hard time... it fills me with shame to think of it now... I simply did whatever it took to grind him down... hurt him... humiliate him... And then, when my guests were leaving – it was after he had gone – I overheard a man saying to his travelling companion: "You know I always had trouble believing the devil was real, until I set eyes on William de Bulmer." His friend laughed. "Aye, I surely know what you mean," he said. I suppose I deserved it. But it didn't feel good. And I was afraid sometimes… that I had lost my humanity… that I was turning into some kind of demon and there would be no way back…'

His caressing hand fell still. 'It was your brother, you know, that made the difference. It was John. He knew precisely what kind of man I was, and what damage I would be capable of doing – and he gave me refuge, not because of what I was but because of what he is. He stood between me and the disgust of the whole community, to save me from the consequences of so many things that had all stacked up against me.'

He twisted to look down at her face. 'If you want to create evil in the world, all you have to do is pick on a little child. Nothing else. That's all you have to do. Because you only have one childhood. You start with an ordinary little lad, and you pick on him relentlessly until you end up with some kind of devil who seeks power over others so that no one will ever, ever treat him that way again. I don't even know I've got free of it now, if I'm honest. I can think of some none too pretty things I've said to you since we were wed. Start again. That's the only thing I can think of to do ever, just start again. Pick myself up and start over when I fall. But the real feeling of shame comes from thinking of the people I've hurt. Seems I'm not big enough to contain it all, let it stop with me, but I must forever be passing it on. I wish… oh, God, I wish I hadn't hurt people like I have.'

The silence between them filled with a sense of sorrow that was of itself so tender and so broken that it seemed to Madeleine to come from some beating heart of life, wider and deeper than just this one man who lay here beside her.

'Madeleine…' he hesitated. Something in her went on alert. This sounded important. 'There's something I've been meaning to ask you, but I haven't been able to pluck up the courage.'

She pulled back to look at him – 'What? What is it?' – and knew it must be something serious when he would not meet her eyes but gazed steadfastly beyond her at the bedpost.

And then, the words tumbling out of him, nervous about how insane this would sound, and how damaging to their plans and hopes of prosperity, he told her about the pigs, described all that Cormac had depicted so vividly. Afraid to look at her, he confessed the truth: that he could not face the prospect of slaughtering any of them – not the runt of the litter for a tasty roast while it was still a milk-fed suckling, nor any of the weaners, nor even a full-grown yearling. None of them.

Listening to him in growing astonishment as she tried to assimilate this ludicrous and completely unexpected proposition, it occurred to Madeleine that she had not been ready for this aspect of marriage. Until now any beast of her flocks had been entirely her own to manage as she wished; as a married woman, she had no property. Everything they owned was in law her husband's, and his to dispose of as he saw fit. She had thought the man she married to be hard-nosed and practical – shrewd and pragmatic, not susceptible to sappy romanticism like this. But if her husband had been seized by some insane desire to turn loose their swine – the best investment they had so far developed and the key-stone of their budget for this year – she had no legal ground for stopping him. He was her lord and master by her own free choice, and there was nothing she could do about it. Even so, too dumbfounded to speak but watching him narrowly as he laid before her his suit for clemency, she saw no sign of arrogance, nothing overbearing. If anything, he reminded her of a brave child at this moment, and the slight tremble in his voice as he made his outrageous proposition did not escape her. Neither did she fail to notice that the notion came to no more than ludicrous sentimentality borrowed from Brother Crazy Cormac; as so she told him when he finished what he had to say, plucked up the courage to look into her eyes for her reaction, and heard her adamant and decided rejection of any such daft proposal. He listened to her thoughtfully, his gaze resting on her face, respectful and quiet, and she thought for a moment she had swayed him. But he said – not argumentatively, nor yet beseechingly, just simply and honestly: 'I asked you before we were married, when you still had time to turn back, did you want the man I am, not just the idea of marriage or of me – and you assured me, yes. Well, this is the man I am. This is what I want to do.'

Madeleine stared at him, nonplussed, the unfamiliar exertion of her efforts at gentle submission not even discarded – just forgotten. 'But… surely there's no need to be so all-or-nothing about it? I can want to be married to you without having to agree to every whim that takes your fancy! Besides, this thing with the pigs is not the man you are; it's the man Brother Cormac is. And no woman alive would want to end up married to him, never mind his blue eyes and his barmy, lop-sided Irish grin.'

William paused on this thought. It had never crossed his mind that these characteristics of Brother Cormac would make him attractive to women, and the idea intrigued him.

'William?' His wife had reared up onto her elbow, and waited with tense anxiety to hear his response. They depended on the pigs, they had built them into their plan for seeing their way clear. Without the pigs, they could manage, but it would be lean and very hard going.

Her husband looked up at her again, his gaze searching hers. So often she saw everything shifting and changing in William's grey-green eyes, as unfathomable and unreadable as sky and sea. They looked different in this moment; very clear and straight.

'It's what I want to do,' he said; and though he spoke softly, something in his tone made Madeleine realize that she, who had never backed down from an argument in all her life, had finally met her match.

'It's the way they are killed,' he added, seeing some further explanation must be necessary. 'Screaming and blood spurting and iron spikes in their snouts. I hadn't thought about it; but now I have, I can't do it. I can't have things terrified and screaming in fear and pain in the place where I live. I can't stand on ground slippery with blood and watch a beast that has trusted me, in pitiful throes as it bleeds to death at my feet. I *can't* do it, Madeleine. I'm sorry. I understand what it means to us, and how important it was to make everything work – well, we'll just have to find another way. I couldn't sit down at my board and eat the flesh of something that died that way – not now I've thought about it. I'm sorry, truly I am. But I can't have any more terror and pain in my life. I don't want to give it houseroom. I don't want anything more to do with it, not in my home. Please... Madeleine – can you not understand?'

'I understand well enough who will have to think up how to make the last of the roots and dried pease get us through – with only the two hens left for eggs, and no goat's milk to speak of! A sucking pig would have done us just nicely! For heaven's sake, William!'

'I know.' As she knelt up on the bed to stare accusingly at her husband, Madeleine saw something vulnerable about his mouth, some trace of horror. He would not meet her eyes now.

'Madeleine,' he whispered, 'it's not that I won't; I *can't*. I can't do it. I can't bear it.' And watching his face, her indignation deflated into numbed acceptance as she realized that he was telling her the simple truth, and she was just going to have to live with it. He really was going to let those pigs go.

'Well, they can run loose with their mother, then,' she said firmly, salvaging what she could, 'for we're not feeding them. They can forage for themselves.'

She saw relief flood his face as he glanced up into her eyes again. 'She... there's not much forage in the woods this time of year,' he ventured, and Madeleine heard something soft and shy in his voice she had never heard before; something she thought maybe had never had a chance until now. 'We can feed her just while they're little and she's suckling them, can't we? She would be so hungry... Madeleine?' The plea in his eyes was naked and desperate.

'Oh! *Saints* and angels! William de Bulmer! *What* are you like? I never heard such soft nonsense in all my born days! Whatever have I married? Do it your own way, then – feed her, cosset her, make a pet of her, and let the whole brood go wild! But, husband – you must take it upon you to make this work. You're the man for the accounts; right then – you do the sums.'

'I will.' He sat up and took her into his arms, drew her down to him again. 'Thank you. I will make it work, somehow I will. Thank you, Madeleine. Thank you so much.'

The gentleness, the tenderness of his kiss made her go weak all over. But she wasn't about to tell him so. He didn't deserve it.

☩   ☩   ☩

'*Dominus vobiscum.*'
　'*Et cum spiritu tuo.*'
　'*Benedicamus Domino.*'
　'*Deo gratias.*'
　'*Fidelium animæ per misericordiam Dei requiescant in pace.*'
　'*Amen.*'

Then the office of None concluded as it always did, with the Pater Noster, and Abbot John left his stall and trailed slowly back along the cloister to his lodging, wishing he was any kind of man in any place on earth other than the superior of a monastic house about to explain to his prior that he intended to give the obedience to somebody else.

He left the door of his house ajar – only a fraction; he was mindful not to be wasteful of the fire's warmth – and drifted uneasily and disconsolately in his atelier, waiting with increasingly heavy heart for his prior's arrival. 'Help me, my Lord Christ,' he whispered. 'Oh, help me of your kindness and your grace. Let me not hurt him. For pity's sake keep watch that I do not destroy him. Help me... please...' The knock at the door came commendably promptly, and John hastened to welcome Father Chad, to offer him a seat at the fireside, and then to properly shut and latch the door, that this cruelty might be carried out with the mercy of close privacy.

'Father,' his prior cut in, before John could say anything, 'I don't know what this is about, but first of all there is something I have to say to you. Will you do me the courtesy of allowing me to get this off my chest before we come on to whatever it is you need to discuss?'

'Of course. Go ahead.' John waited with surprise for what Father Chad had to tell him. The prior looked agitated. Evidently this was something of urgency and importance.

'Well... this is something that has been on my heart for a long time now. I've been meaning to tell you about it, but just haven't been able to make myself do it. I've thought it all through carefully, again and again, and it goes right back to when Father Columba fell ill. Before he came to us, during Abbot Gregory's time, things were simple here. Our house is remote up here in the hills, and we had no special reputation; we attracted few vocations. With Father Columba, all that changed. He had such charisma, and such high standards, I began to feel myself wading in deeper water than my capabilities allowed. But even then it was not too bad. A prior, after all, has only to do the bidding of his abbot. The obedience asks patience and kindness, discretion and meticulous care in carrying out an assignment, not much more.

'Then Father Abbot fell sick, and everything changed again. In his long incapacity, decisions were needed that were more than I was equal to. I think I made mistakes. I could feel myself becoming unpopular. I began to realize that some of the brothers actually held me in contempt. I was a figure of fun sometimes. There were relationships – with Brother Thomas, for instance – that got worse and worse no matter what I did. It was dreadful, sometimes, with Brother Thomas…' The prior shook his head, lost in the appalling memory of it.

'When that long interregnum finally reached an end, and you came to take up the abbacy, I felt so relieved. I thought everything would go back to normal again. But then hot on your heels William de Bulmer arrived. I did what I could, Father, I promise you I did, I give you my word: but the evident scorn with which he regarded me undermined me completely. I found myself, against my own better judgment, posturing and defensive and argumentative, resenting him and bearing a grudge. I found that the way I carried out my tasks got emptier and emptier – until I had lost any sense of authenticity, and was just clinging to rank and position for the false comfort it confers. I was almost more angry with him than I was capable of containing. I nursed the bitterest grudge against him. Worse than that, I encouraged Brother Ambrose in following my example; and before God I hope his soul was clean of that when he breathed his last.

'When Father William left here so suddenly, and I realized I wouldn't have to live with him any more after all, I thought it would be all right. I thought I could take my time to recover my equilibrium and find a way to fill what was required of me as this community's prior. I never expected that he would be back. It was the profoundest shock to encounter him, here at your table, and learn that he would be meddling about in our affairs yet again. Father, I loathe him. I confess to you, I absolutely detest that man.

'I am willing to make confession of this in Chapter. I am ashamed that I cannot find so much as a scrap of charity to extend towards him, however deep I dig.

'The thing is that he himself seems to neither like nor dislike me. He just ignores me, unless he is obliged to speak to me. He bypasses me. He looks straight through me. And I am forced to conclude that the problem is my pride. I'm not – I'm not taking too long about this am I, Father John?'

'No… er… no!' responded his abbot. 'No – please carry on.'

'A proud prior is like a dangerous disease. The obedience is too high a position. In our holy Rule it makes most clear that any prior blinded by vainglory should be removed from his position if he cannot overcome his sin with admonishment. Oh, Father, I have tried and tried and tried! And at last I can see no other course. I have come to beg you, of your charity, may I not lay this obedience down? It has grown too heavy for me. It is greater than the man I am. It has become a Saul's armour to me, impeding my every step. Unless I can go back into some less exalted position, I fear I may lose my vocation and even my faith. Please, Father; won't you let me do something quiet and ordinary, so that I can do the soul work that is necessary to find my way to simplicity again, and charity, and peace?

'I felt so shamed in my spirit when I saw how Brother Thomas was able to embrace William de Bulmer with an honest heart; and he even came to love him in the end – I believe he really did. But not me. Will you allow it, Father? Will you let me lay this down? It is too much for me!'

'Ssh!' John leaned forward kindly and touched Father Chad's knee, interrupting the flow of words. Trembling and on the verge of tears, the prior raised a shaking hand to his brow, overcome by the terrible nature of what he had to confess.

'First, let me say – of course you may lay this down,' said the abbot. 'You have carried the task manfully these many years. A change will do you the world of good, I'm sure. Second, let me assure you that William de Bulmer has no smooth path in any form of companionship. As animosity has yoked the two of you together, please pray for him. Love him in that act of kindness if you can love him in no other way. He will not be much longer in our midst. Just let him get Brother Cormac through the challenges of the Lady Day rents, the Easter Triduum, and the bishop's Visitation, and he will need to come here only very occasionally as our guest. Had it not been for my mismanagement he would not have had to come back here at all – but he has been gracious in his help; try to remember that. If he sets your teeth on edge, well, just offer it up; we cannot all find a way to comfortable friendship.

'Rest at ease, my good brother, we can deal with this. I will tell them in Chapter tomorrow, and you can lay this down. Have a little think about where best you might like to serve – in the sacristy, maybe? Do you think that would suit you? And in the library? And maybe I could imagine you doing a bit of gardening – getting brown in the sunshine. Think it through and let me know.'

Father Chad's shaking hand subsided into his lap, and John saw calm gradually restoring in his expression.

'Thank you.' He sounded tired and forlorn. 'Yes, I think it might be peaceful to work in the library. I should love to do that. And the idea of the sacristy does sound nice as well, I must say. And the garden. Oh, Father, I am not proud of myself. And to let you down like this, when you have been in office for only a year. Who will you find to serve as prior in my stead? Who is there among us with the stature the obedience requires? I don't know. I just don't know…'

'We'll find someone,' said Abbot John, his voice quiet and comforting. 'Father Francis, perhaps.'

'Francis?' The erstwhile obedientiary's head jerked up in consternation. 'Father Francis is almost as flighty as the day he entered! You can't ask him!'

John smiled. 'Concentrate on how Christ is calling and leading you, Father,' he said gently, 'and trust the appointment of prior into my hands. It will be well. I think God is watching over us. He knows our condition; he is merciful. And I think he may have a sense of humour, as well as that.'

This far to the north of England the sun set early in February, only an hour after None. When Father Chad left the abbot's lodging, the crushing anxiety he had been carrying when he arrived not rivalled even by his consternation about the prospect of Francis as prior of St Alcuin's when he left, the sun had spread a pageant of crimson and violet across the western sky.

Abbot John reached down for the fire irons and pushed the smouldering logs together, blew on them a while to revive a flame. Then he sat back in his chair in the quietness of the day, reviewing the way they had come, the changes made.

'Thank you,' he whispered, thinking of Father Chad. 'Thank you so much.'

The day drew to its close. Soon it would be time for Vespers, and supper. The evening folded around him with its breath of peace.

The story of the monks of
St Alcuin's continues in

The Beautiful Thread

Glossary of Terms

Bradawl – a tool with a wooden handle and a metal spike. Old norse origins to the word.

Cellarer – monk responsible for oversight of all provisions; a key role in the community.

Chapter – daily meeting governing practical matters, where a chapter of St Benedict's Rule was read and expounded by the abbot.

Checker – a small, separate building, in the part of the monastery accessible to laypeople, where all the documents of trade (receipts, account books, etc.) were kept, and where tradespeople could be received. The word *exchequer* comes from this.

Choir – the part of the church where the community sits.

Cloister – covered way giving access to main buildings of a monastery.

Corrody – purchased right to food/clothing/housing from a monastery for an agreed period, which could be for life.

Frater – refectory.

Grafter – worker.

Gong – the pile of human dung accumulating, in most cases on the ground outside from a long-drop toilet above.

Grand Silence – the silence kept by the whole community from after Compline when they retired for the night until after first Mass in the morning.

Jakes – dung pile (as 'gong'), or compost toilet.

Morrow Mass – the first of two daily celebrations of the Mass, this one being smaller and more intimate than the later one open to the wider public.

Nave – the body of the church occupied by the public in worship.

Obedientiary – monk assigned to a specific role in his community.

Office – the set worship taking place at regular intervals through the day.

Palfrey – high-bred riding horse.

Pease – medieval form of 'peas' that meant dried legumes in general.

Porridge – English term for oatmeal cooked with milk and/or water.

Postulant – person aspiring to join the community, living in the monastery in the stage of commitment preceding entry into the novitiate.

Pottage – a thick soup or stew made with anything available – vegetables, grains, meat, poultry, fish – added to and varied as the days went by.

Rule – the Benedictine Rule is the document in which St Benedict set out the way of life for his monks to follow. A monk would say he lives not by rules but by a Rule – a guidance for a way to live, not an inflexible set of regulations.

Runkling – the runt of the litter, the smallest animal in a birth group.

Vielle – a bowed stringed instrument similar to a violin but with five strings. One of the most popular European musical instruments through the thirteenth to fifteenth centuries.

Warming room – the place in a medieval monastery that served as a common room. It had a big fireplace.

Monastic Day

There may be slight variation from place to place and at different times from the Dark Ages through the Middle Ages and onwards – e.g., Vespers may be after supper rather than before. This gives a rough outline. Slight liberties are taken in my novels to allow human interactions to play out.

Winter Schedule (from Michaelmas)
2:30 a.m. Preparation for the nocturns of matins – psalms, etc.

3:00 a.m. Matins, with prayers for the royal family and for the dead.

5:00 a.m. Reading in preparation for Lauds.

6:00 a.m. Lauds at daybreak and Prime; wash and break fast (just bread and water, standing).

8:30 a.m. Terce, Morrow Mass, Chapter.

12:00 noon Sext, Sung Mass, midday meal.

2:00 p.m. None.

4:15 p.m. Vespers, Supper, Collatio.

6:15 p.m. Compline.

The Grand Silence begins.

Summer Schedule
1:30 a.m. Preparation for the nocturns of matins – psalms etc.

2:00 a.m. Matins.

3:30 a.m. Lauds at daybreak, wash and break fast.

6:00 a.m. Prime, Morrow Mass, Chapter.

8:00 a.m. Terce, Sung Mass.

11:30 a.m. Sext, midday meal.

2:30 p.m. None.

5:30 p.m. Vespers, Supper, Collatio.

8:00 p.m. Compline.

The Grand Silence begins.

Liturgical Calendar

I have included the main feasts and fasts in the cycle of the church's year, plus one or two other dates that are mentioned (e.g., Michaelmas and Lady Day when rents were traditionally collected) in these stories.

Advent – begins four Sundays before Christmas.

Christmas – December 25th.

Holy Innocents – December 28th.

Epiphany – January 6th.

Baptism of our Lord concludes Christmastide, Sunday after January 6th.

Candlemas – February 2nd (Purification of Blessed Virgin Mary, Presentation of Christ in the temple).

Lent – Ash Wednesday to Holy Thursday – start date varies with phases of the moon.

Holy Week – last week of Lent and the Easter Triduum.

Easter Triduum (three days) of Good Friday, Holy Saturday, Easter Sunday.

Lady Day – March 25th – this was New Year's Day between 1155 and 1752.

Ascension – forty days after Easter.

Whitsun (Pentecost) – fifty days after Easter.

Trinity Sunday – Sunday after Pentecost.

Corpus Christi – Thursday after Trinity Sunday.

Sacred Heart of Jesus – Friday of the following week.

Feast of John the Baptist – June 24th.

Lammas (literally 'loaf-mass'; grain harvest) – August 1st.

Michaelmas – feast of St Michael and All Angels, September 29th.

All Saints – November 1st.

All Souls – November 2nd.

Martinmas – November 11th.